C000255037

The adventures of
Devon - Revisited

The adventures of Bella & Emily Devon-Revisited

Week 1

* * *

Michelle Lesley Holland

MLHolland

Holland 2019
All rights reserved
No part of this publication may be reproduced, stored in a retrieval system, or transmitted in
any form or by any means, without the prior permission in writing of Michelle Holland, nor
be otherwise circulated in any form of binding or cover other than that in which it is published
and without a similar condition including this condition being imposed on the subsequent
purchaser.

Cover design by Sam Wall

This book is dedicated to my Mum, Sonya Holland and to my dear friend Ena Webster.
My Mum always inspired me to follow my dreams and Ena supported and encouraged me to
write my books. I am very sad that neither are no longer with us. They are both a big part of my
books, and their memory will live on.

I would also like to make a special mention to Steph Lewis for inspiring me to write this book.
Thank you also to Hannah, Jan and Dee for all your help.

Typeset by Amnet Systems

50% OF ANY PROFIT FROM THE SALE OF THIS BOOK WILL BE DONATED BETWEEN ANIMAL RESCUE CHARITIES AND ORGANISATIONS OF MY CHOICE.

Chapter 1

I HONESTLY CANNOT TELL YOU how excited I am. Today is Sunday the third of August and once again I am on my way to visit Aunty Pam accompanied by my beautiful pony Bella.

So much has happened since my visit to Aunty's in April this year and I have approximately three hours to update you, before we arrive back in Devon.

Where shall I start?

I know, let's start at the very beginning, a very good place to start! (This is what my Nan says to me when I get too excited).

You will remember, my last visit was a bit of a whirlwind and once I arrived home, I cannot tell you how much I missed Flax, Speckle, Aunty Pam and her gang. I know Bella missed the company of her new friends too, so we both tried to keep as busy as we possibly could.

The weekend after we got home, Bella and I were thrilled to hear Sophie and Flash wanted to come and stay. We were delighted to see them again and Bella & Flash had a wonderful time prancing, flirting and chasing each other around the paddock, acting as though they hadn't seen each other in years.

Sophie and I also had so much to catch up on. I literally spent hours telling her about our fabulous week away and as I told her chapter by chapter, I felt as though I was reliving my adventures with Bella in Devon all over again. My excitement and enthusiasm proved to be very infectious to Sophie as there and then we started to plan our sponsored ride in aid of Aunty Pam's rescues.

I'd arranged a meeting for me and Sophie with Mrs Evans, the riding school owner at four o'clock on Saturday. We took the long scenic route by riding across the glorious South Downs, laughing, joking and racing against each other in the beautiful April sunshine. Bella and Flash kept kissing each other like long lost friends.

I hate being late and as you are aware Mrs Evans does not tolerate lateness, so much to my relief we arrived with just five minutes to spare.

Mrs Evans as always was thrilled to see all four of us and after two hours of intense discussions, we'd finally agreed on a day and time to hold our sponsored ride. The distance would be eight miles across the stunning South Downs. Saturday the fourteenth of June was the day we had finally decided on.

I seriously hadn't realised how much time and hard work was required in organising an event like this. There was so much to think about and a list of jobs to do that seemed endless.

Thankfully Mrs Evans already had insurance so that was easily solved. The three of us did a risk assessment and rode over the route at least five times on the run up to our event, to ensure the bridleways on the route were clear and safe.

Out of courtesy, Sophie made a visit to all the local farmers to inform them of our event. Thankfully there were no objections at all, in fact everyone seemed totally supportive.

We also had to find ten stewards. It was essential to have two at the start, one at every mile marker and another at the finish.

Something very important which I would never have thought of, was the need to make sure at every single marker where a steward was going to be, that they had a strong mobile signal. This was essential, in case any of them needed to call for help in an emergency.

Our local St John Ambulance unit also agreed to attended but thankfully we didn't need to use any of their expertise.

The day of the ride was warm and thankfully not too hot. A few fluffy white clouds danced around in the bright blue sky, ideal conditions for our event.

The day before, Sophie and I had ridden the route one final time. We were very excited and chatted continuously as we merrily dropped off the markers at the required points. We'd also double checked the mobile networks were still giving out a strong signal.

Freya, my friend who you will remember from Devon proved to be a great help promoting our event and appealing for sponsors on Aunty Pam's Facebook page.

I was also overjoyed to see almost everyone at Mrs Evans's riding school had got involved to support our wonderful cause. Some of the Mums even made cakes to sell alongside hot and cold drinks. I must say Mrs Evans was truly buzzing on the day and much to my relief, she had applied her lipstick perfectly. She was in her element as she ran around organising everyone and making sure everything was ship shape.

Sophie and I had arrived at seven am with Bella and Flash who as always were looking truly magnificent with their shiny summer coats.

The ride commenced at nine and the riders were staggered in small groups with fifteen-minute gaps. We were absolutely overwhelmed with the number of entries. Forty-eight had registered online and had already paid the minimum ten pounds entry fee and another twenty-nine turned up on the day. Sophie and I were on cloud nine as we set off leading the way in very high spirits.

It was very important for us to get back to the riding school in plenty of time as Sophie and I were presenting every rider with a beautiful red rosette which I may add cost us absolutely nothing. We had managed to get the cost of them sponsored by our local Estate Agent.

On our calculations, with a horse walking on average four miles per hour, the ride would take between an hour and an hour and a half to complete. Children under twelve were required to be accompanied by an adult and everyone who took part had a truly magnificent time.

Sophie and I completed the ride in just under fifty minutes, as by this time our ponies knew the route only too well. Bella knew exactly when we weren't far from the finishing line, as she'd continuously pranced, danced, and snorted with excitement. I'd stroked her with a huge grin on my face.

Once we had completed our ride, we'd quickly turned Flash and Bella out into one of the spare paddocks. They'd immediately got down to have a good old roll. I smiled at Sophie as we watched our babies roll to the left to the right, stand up, get down and repeat it all over again.

Sophie and I were beaming proudly as we presented each rider their well-deserved rosette.

The biggest horse to take part had been a stunning Irish draught mare called Delora. Can you believe she stood at a whopping 17.1hh? I'd seriously had to stand on my tip toes to pat this magnificent specimen of a horse. The smallest contestant on the day was one of the cutest Shetland Ponies I have ever seen. He was called Honey Bear and stood at only 10.1hh. His proud little owner Molly who was only eight years old, couldn't stop grinning. The photo I took of Delora and Honey Bear (Little and large we nicknamed them) standing side by side with their rosettes, received over one thousand likes on Aunty Pam's Facebook page.

By four o'clock everyone had gone home, so Sophie and I sat down with a well-deserved cup of coffee in Mrs Evans's kitchen, counting out the money. The seventy-seven entries had brought in an amazing seven hundred and seventy pounds.

Here is an unexpected bonus we certainly weren't expecting. Some of the riders had manged to get in private sponsorship money. Not only did this put a massive smile on our faces, it gave us extra money to add into the pot. Sophie and I were speechless when we realized we had another five-hundred and twenty pounds to add to the total.

The cakes and refreshments made an amazing seventy-two pounds and thirty pence and Freya's appeals for online sponsorship gave us another three-hundred and forty-two pounds from Aunty Pam's Rescue page supporters.

Drum roll please. The grand total for our sponsored ride was, one thousand, eight hundred and four pounds and thirty pence.

I bet you have a massive grin on your face now.

The seven weeks of endless hard work, and planning, had finally paid off.

Later that afternoon, Sophie and I skyped Aunty Pam knowing Freya was by her side. Yes, you have guessed right there were many, many tears of joy flowing down Aunty's face. A definite resemblance to a waterfall.

Thankfully Freya had a box of tissues to hand as I'd messaged her earlier with the total, and we both knew only too well how Aunty would react when we told her.

After the tears had stopped, Aunty did a very bizarre thing. Would you believe in all her excitement, she actually picked up the computer screen from her desk, planted a kiss straight onto Sophie' left cheek and within seconds I had received one of her virtual kisses directly onto my forehead. As you can imagine, this was then followed by a massive outburst of laughter from both sides of the screen.

Once Aunty had calmed down, she told us the money we'd raised in April had nearly all gone. Our foals had all been gelded but unfortunately poor Shadow had developed an infection not long after and was prescribed a very strong course of antibiotics. The castrations ended up costing a lot more than she had initially budgeted for.

Our sponsored ride had most definitely come at the right time for Aunty and her rescues.

Chapter 2

✳ ✳ ✳

"EMILY, COULD YOU DO ME a huge favour? Would you mind pouring me a cup of coffee from my flask please? Feel free to help yourself to one too", asks Laura, momentarily interrupting my story-telling.

"Of course, I will", I reply.

I turn around and wink at Bella.

"Hey baby girl, how are you doing?" I ask her with a big grin on my face.

Bella immediately responds by nodding her head up and down whilst letting out a little whinny.

I am sure my baby is half human.

Thankfully the motorway is running smoothly, and we are now over half way to Auntys.

"I wonder what adventures you and Bella are going to get up to on this visit Emily?" laughs Laura.

'I know one thing for sure. I am going to be very busy with my assignment', I reply smiling to myself as I think of all the quality time Speckle and I will be spending together.

One thing I haven't told you yet, is that Aunty had called me on the seventh of July to let me know Bev had received a serious enquiry about Flax. She'd already carried out the home check too. I will tell you now, my heart sank heavily when I heard these words, and an overwhelming moment of sadness had totally engulfed me. I could not stop the tears as they rolled down my face.

The potential home was in Cornwall. The lady who is called Sam had adopted a pony from Aunty around four years ago. She had achieved amazing results with Josh, a 13.2hh New Forest Pony who had originally arrived at Aunty's in an appalling state. Josh had been found by some walkers tethered to the ground by a chain which was around his neck. He'd had no access to either water or shelter. The winter that year had been very harsh and poor Josh had suffered severe rain scald. His body had been covered with crusty scabs and lesions.

Val had raced as quickly as she possibly could to get to where poor Josh had been found with the vet following in hot pursuit. Can you believe, once again there was no microchip? He was very under-weight as the grazing was more mud than grass. He had no access to water and needed immediate veterinary attention. The animal wel-fare team were immediately called in and that is how Josh had ended up at Auntys.

Adam, who is Aunty's vet had taken various samples from the scabs so he could investigate further by taking a closer look under his microscope. This had enabled him to finally be able to prescribe the correct treatment Josh so desperately needed. He'd said with rain scald there are always many different types of bacteria involved.

Six months on from his ordeal, Josh had been ready to find his forever home and at only five years old, Aunty knew it wouldn't be too difficult. He had a very willing attitude along with enormous potential.

Aunty had then continued to tell me more about Sam.

Sam is a professional animal healer and when they adopted Josh, their son Luke was only thirteen years old. With lots of schooling and preparation, Josh turned into one fabulous all-round pony, winning show jumping classes, gymkhana's and even excelled at pony club. Sam is only five foot two inches herself, and regularly rides him too. Luke is going to college in September and Sam was worried Josh may get lonesome which is why she'd enquired about Flax.

Aunty said it was love at first sight for all of them. After the family had spent lots of time with Flax, everyone was totally thrilled when the paperwork was signed, and he finally went to his Forever home on the twenty fourth of July.

I have seen the photos on Aunty's Facebook page of Flax, and I have to say he does look very happy and settled in his new home alongside his new brother Josh. I am truly happy for him, but at the same time I feel sad, if that makes sense. As you are aware, Flax stole a very large piece of my heart, but like Freya says, what is meant to be, will be.

"Forty minutes away", smiles Laura.

I am starting to get butterflies in my tummy again. I can't wait to see Aunty Pam and her gang.

Aunty has recently taken in more additions, but she wouldn't tell me anything more on the phone. She had just laughed and told me to be patient as I would meet them soon enough!

I have some more good news to tell you. Do you remember our two foals, Shadow the gorgeous little bay and Fern the stunning strawberry roan? They've both been reserved subject to home checks.

How amazing is this?

"Twenty minutes away", Laura informs me.

I quickly text Aunty and Mum.

Mum had been running around frantically in the early hours of this morning double checking I had everything I needed. I had started packing over a week ago and as I am staying for three weeks this time, I decided to bring two suit cases full of clothes, although I doubt, I shall wear them all.

I nearly forgot to tell you. Freya has a boyfriend and I am looking forward to meeting him. He is called Jamie and according to Freya, apparently, he looks like a younger version of Joseph.

You must remember Joseph?

Aunty's good friend who Freya has a crush on.

Really?

Chapter 3

* * *

A HUGE SMILE CROSSES MY face as I bounce around in my seat like a rubber ball along the familiar bumpy road gripping as tightly as I can to my seat. I remember this road only too well from last time and I am thrilled when at last we make it around the tight right-hand bend. I can see Aunty's house in the distance and relax my grip.

"Bella, we are nearly here", I gush in excitement.

The familiar black iron gates slowly start to open, and I laugh to myself as I watch Aunty jumping up and down like a kangaroo whilst waving frantically at the same time. I can see Molly and Tinker by her side and another person is running towards the horsebox.

I cannot believe it. Freya is here too.

I try to be patient as the horsebox comes to a halt and the engine stops. Bella releases a huge whinny. She must know where we are. I release my seat belt as fast as I can and jump out quickly but unfortunately in all the excitement, I have somehow misjudged the step down and now seem to be sitting on my backside. I glance up to see Aunty and Freya laughing at me very loudly.

"Welcome back Ems", says Aunty as she holds out a hand to help me up, followed by a massive hug that nearly takes my breath away.

"My turn Ems", laughs Freya as she wraps her arms around me too.

I can feel something very familiar poking my backside. I slowly turn around to see Aunty's gorgeous little pygmy goat, Tinker. I kneel-down and plant a little kiss on top of his gorgeous little head.

"You remember me little fella?" I ask him.

I think he is saying yes. He mutters a little bleat and is poking his tiny tongue out at me.

Before I have a chance to stand up, within seconds I am on my backside once again. I have literally been ambushed by Molly, Lexy, Moss and Sugar. I seem to have four excited doggie tongues licking my face and four wriggling bodies on top of my poor body.

Laura cannot contain her laughter.

"Now that is what I call a proper welcome", she grins.

Once again, whilst trying to stifle her giggles, Aunty offers her hand to pull me up off the floor.

I brush myself down and take a deep breath. I have a feeling this is going to be a very fun filled, three weeks.

Freya is busy helping Laura unload the hay and my suitcases whilst Aunty rushes to put the dogs and Tinker inside the house until we have got Bella settled in.

The ramp is down. I walk up towards Bella, she lets out another soft and gentle whinny and my heart soars with love for her.

We make our way slowly down the ramp. Bella stops half way down and slowly moves her head around to look at the familiar breath-taking views. Her eyes are wide open with excitement. She most definitely knows where we are. Her head is high in the air. Another enormous whinny emerges, her beautiful nostrils are open wide, flaring in and out as she calls to her friends.

In the far distance I can hear some of the others whinnying back. "Wowzee", says Freya.

"I nearly didn't recognise Bella, Ems. She has completely changed colour. Look at her beautiful golden coat. How amazing is that?" she continues.

"Well, well, well Bella. Just look at you. You are now a golden Princess. Welcome back my darling", says Aunty as she gently plants a kiss on her velvety soft muzzle.

Bella lets out a huge contented sigh before plopping her head heavily over Aunty's shoulder!

"Hey guys, I need to get going. I hope you and Bella have a fabulous time Ems and I will see you three weeks today. I am sure you are going to have plenty to tell me when I come to take you and Bella home", says Laura.

"Thank you so much Laura. Have a safe journey home", I reply.

We all wave Laura off and watch as the black iron gates finally close.

Bella is getting impatient. She is pawing her front left hoof on the ground. I am sure she is desperate to see her friends again.

"Come on. Let's get Bella settled in the field with her friends so she can stretch her legs. We can sort out the hay and suitcases later after we have had a nice cuppa", informs Aunty.

Bella is walking at a very eager pace and I try my hardest to get her to slow down a little.

Freya, Bella and I follow Aunty around to the right of the house. My heart skips a beat.

Once again, the beauty of the old cobbled stables gazes back at me capturing my attention. The flowers around the yard are in full bloom, the colours of the petals look beautiful and mesmerising.

Loud whinnies to the left make me gaze over to see Amber and Crystal with their stunning heads over their stable door welcoming us back. I have the biggest and silliest grin across my face. I cannot tell you how happy I am feeling at this precise moment to be back here.

I glance over to the stables and corral where the foals used to be. The paddock stands completely empty and I notice the bottom doors to the stables are closed and bolted.

Aunty is watching me.

"You don't miss anything, do you Ems. I will tell you everything later", she smiles.

Bella is jogging along and snorting in excitement as I try to lean my body against hers to slow her down.

I look ahead to see many heads popping over the main gate to the field. Aunty and Freya go ahead to move the ponies away, so Bella and I can get in safely.

Nearly there.

As I approach the gate, I notice Aunty and Freya are in the centre of the field scattering what must be pony nuts to keep them all busy. Bella and I nip quickly through the gate. I remove her head collar and lead rope and watch with sheer delight as she quickly turns and canters off. She is whinnying louder than I have ever heard her do so since I have owned her. Within seconds I can see many ponies with their heads held high in the air.

Bella is prancing and snorting. Hope cannot believe her eyes. Whilst whinnying loudly in excitement, she goes from a complete standstill to a canter within a split second. She is heading at full speed across the field directly towards Bella.

It doesn't take long before I notice, I can see at least twelve beautiful ponies galloping around the field in complete unison. What a truly magical sight to see. Freya and Aunty have made their way safely back to the gate. The three of us stand smiling, watching in awe at this tremendous display the ponies are putting on for us.

Chapter 4

* * *

I AM COMPLETELY TAKEN BY surprise when Speckle drops out of the chasing game and I hold my breath as she walks towards the gate and comes to a standstill about twelve feet away from me.

"Hey baby girl. You won't believe how good it is to see you. Do you remember me?" I ask her in a very soft voice.

I truly cannot believe what happens next. Speckle lets out a very soft and gentle whinny and takes two steps forward. Freya very slowly hands me her bum bag and I take two steps forward keeping my head low. I quickly look around and I am relieved to see the others have settled down to eat at the far end of the field.

I turn my back and slowly sit down on the grass with my head hanging as low as it will go. Aunty and Freya have moved far away from the gate.

Within seconds I can feel the familiar touch of a gentle muzzle ruffling tenderly through my hair. As slowly as I can I put my left hand into the bum bag and hold a handful of nuts out for her. I am totally taken aback to see Speckle is now standing directly in front of me. I slowly lift my head and for a moment our eyes are locked together. The true understanding and connection we had in April is still there. I feel on cloud nine. Speckle hasn't forgotten me.

For a moment I have so many emotions running through my body, it is so hard to explain. Love, trust and understanding spring to mind.

Speckle leans further towards me. She doesn't want the nuts, instead she tenderly licks my right hand. Her tongue is warm, soft and gentle.

"Good girlie, that is so kind of you", I tell her.

Speckle slowly moves her mouth over to my left hand and starts to nibble on the nuts. It is like we are locked in our own tiny little bubble, in a world of our own. I slowly lift my right hand to stroke her under her chin. She doesn't move. As calmly as I can, I make a move to stand up. Speckle doesn't move. I load my left hand with more nuts and slowly move my right hand as gently as I can onto her neck. She still doesn't move. I lean my body against hers. I am as close to her than I have ever been. I can even feel her heart beating.

At this very moment I feel emotional and very honoured to have this special trust and bond with Speckle.

I am suddenly brought out of this truly magical moment by a prod to my back. Speckle slowly takes a step sideways. I turn to see Bella who without hesitation plops her head over my right shoulder.

"Oh, there you are my beautiful Bella. I hope you weren't jealous?" I ask her with a smile on my face as I wrap my arms tightly around her neck.

Bella sighs back contentedly until Hope whinnies to her. She suddenly spins around and gallops back to her friends.

I slowly turn to see Speckle is watching me from a distance. I blow her a kiss.

"See you later on my darling", I call to her.

I hadn't realised Aunty and Freya had been watching Speckle and I all this time.

"Ems, you have the most amazing connection with Speckle. To be honest I have never seen anything like it", smiles Aunty.

"I tried to connect with Speckle Ems, just like you asked me to, but she wasn't having any of it. Every time I tried to get anywhere near her, she would just snort and trot away", says Freya.

"I must say I am truly excited about my assignment on behaviour and horse welfare for my level three Diploma in equine management. I have only thirteen months left of my two-year course and I have already completed forty per cent. This work placement and work experience is going to really help my marks Aunty. I can't thank you enough for letting me and Bella come to stay", I say humbly.

"Ems, the pleasure is all mine. The help and support you give me is priceless. The college have asked me to write a report and send it to your tutor when you have completed your three weeks here. I wonder what else I am going to be able to add?" laughs Aunty.

"Wow Ems. I am so proud of you. I hate to admit it, but I am really struggling with level two, especially the introduction to lunging and equine anatomy section. Thankfully your Aunty has been pointing me in the right direction and we have done quite a few hours in the school lunging Hope and at long last my confidence is growing. I completed my one hundred and fifty hours of work placement by at least a hundred hours, but I am still not over confident on some aspects of equine health and welfare", blurts out Freya without even stopping for a breath.

"Freya, I am more than happy to spend time with you going through my notes on equine health and welfare. I did get a very strong mark in my assignment and would feel honoured to help you if I can".

"Really?" gasps Freya.

"Of course. That's what friends are for", I reply.

With big grins across our faces we turn to look at Aunty who I swear has a tear in her eye.

After we'd finished moving Bella's hay to the feed room and I'd unpacked my suitcases, Aunty put the kettle on and at last it was time to sit down and have a good old catch up.

"Aunty, what is it you have been waiting to tell me?" I ask.

"Well Ems, as you know Sooty went to his new home and so did Flax. Both are doing incredibly well. We have a wonderful family who have been working with Jet and the fabulous news is he is now reserved. He will be leaving us to go to his new home on Tuesday. He has been doing incredibly well with the regular schooling and training I have been doing with him since you left. I am thrilled to tell you that two weeks ago after numerous times spent lunging him in a saddle, our Freya here sat on him for the first time. He behaved like the perfect gentleman he is", says Aunty beaming.

"Oh Ems, you are going to love his new family. They have a wonderful son called Jake who is twelve years old. He has now out-grown his first pony Jude who is only 12.2hh and sixteen years old. Jake has competed on Jude since the age of six and he has lovely kind hands and such a wonderful energy about him. His Mum is a riding instructor and has a 16.0hh Irish hunter they have three acres of land and it was love at first sight when they all met", pipes up Freya full of excitement.

"That is absolutely fabulous news. I am so thrilled for Jet and his new family', I beam back.

Chapter 5

* * *

"Aunty, I am sure I counted twelve ponies cantering around the field and on my calculations, there should be only ten?" I query.

"Spot on Ems. We have Shady and Benny staying with us until next week. I rescued them both around four years ago. Their owners had to go away to Australia at very short notice for three weeks, so I said they could stay here with us. Their family have made a very large donation of three hundred pounds", smiles Aunty.

"Ems, Benny is very comical and Shady is one of the cheekiest ponies I have every met. Last week as I was bending over to poo pick the field, Shady crept up behind me, started to rub his head up and down on my backside, I lost my balance and fell flat on my face into a fresh pile of dung", says Freya grimacing.

I cannot help but laugh out loud as I picture this in my head and Aunty joins in too.

'It doesn't finish there Ems. Once I had scrambled to my feet, I swear Shady was laughing at me as he put his top lip in the air, and had the cheek to get down and roll around in the fresh dung I had just landed in. His head was covered in poo, just like mine. Honestly what a pair we must have looked", she laughs.

"That is very funny Freya", I giggle back.

"I then had to wash the dung off Shady. I must say he thoroughly enjoyed all the attention, maybe that is why he did it in the first place. Who knows? I couldn't wait to get back home and jump into the shower", continues Freya.

"Shady and Benny are such a pair of characters. They came to me after being found wandering around the roads in a little village in Cornwall. They were slightly underweight, needed a visit from the farrier and some worming treatment but to be honest apart from that they weren't in too bad a condition. Shady is only 11.0hh and twelve years old. Benny is slightly shorter at 10.2hh and is now fourteen years old. We ran appeals within a sixty-mile radius to find their owners but to no avail. No microchips once again. They were and still are a friendly and loving pair of lads. I think they must have been outgrown by their owners and just dumped as I am sure at some point in their lives they have lived with a family", says Aunty.

"Poor little guys", I reply.

"They are not anymore Ems. Their adopted family give them the very best of everything. I can promise you, they never want for anything. Liz, their Mum even allows them to wander freely around the inside of their farmhouse", smiles Aunty.

"How awesome is that? I can't wait to meet them properly", I respond.

I get up to place my empty cup into the sink and I am convinced for one second, I can hear the voice of a donkey. In fact, I am sure I can, and it doesn't seem to be coming from too far away.

Freya and Aunty both laugh.

"Oh yes Ems, we have so much more to tell you", grins Aunty.

"We have someone we want you to meet", she continues.

I look at Freya for a clue, but she just smiles, as I follow them out to the stables where the foals used to reside.

"Pop your head over the far stable door Ems", Aunty urges.

I walk slowly across the yard, not knowing what I am going to see. I let out a gasp as I see the most beautiful little donkey I have ever seen. A pure white snowy colour all over, apart from a little black star between his/her eyes. My heart is instantly filled with love.

'Eeyore', the donkey says to me in a very sweet way.

"Go on Ems, in you go. Meet Snowy. Snowy meet Ems", smiles Aunty.

I open the bolt and the kick-latch and slowly make my way in, closely followed by Aunty and Freya.

"Hello, my little man", I whisper to him.

I kneel next to him in the thick straw bed and he instantly leans his little head forward to sniff my left cheek. His breath is warm, and his whiskers tickle my face. He has the biggest almond shape brown eyes I have ever seen, along with stunning, long black eyelashes.

"Ems, if you look very closely you will see he has the very faint cross of Jesus under his coat. Freya, do you want to tell Ems all about Snowy's rescue mission?" asks Aunty.

"I would love to. Your Aunty got a call from Val around six weeks ago to say a donkey had been found in the corner of an old wooden building about fifty miles from here. A small pony who had sadly passed away was laying by his side. The vet who was on the scene estimated the deceased pony to be quite old and could have been lay-ing there for around five days. An old barrel of filthy rusty water had been standing in the corner of the derelict building. Snowy was not only grieving from the loss of his friend, he was also in an enormous amount of pain. His hooves had curled up so badly he was unable to walk. The vet reckoned his hooves had not been trimmed in at least two years. This meant his legs could not sit properly on the ground which caused a knock-on effect to his bones, muscles and joints. His hooves were so over grown and curled up by at least ten inches, which isn't far off the size of a standard ruler. Due to him not being able to walk properly, he was also suffering from malnutrition as he was unable to walk far to graze", Freya informs me.

My eyes instantly well up and I can feel a lump in my throat as I picture this all in my head.

"Your Aunt obviously agreed to take him in immediately and once again no microchip was found. Val has been busy trying to find out more information about him but to date nothing has emerged. No-one seems to know anything. The vet sedated Snowy and thinks he is only around six years old. He gave him very strong painkillers to keep him as comfortable as possible on his journey here. Honestly Ems, when we saw him try and hobble down the ramp of the trailer our hearts went straight out to him and we both couldn't help but shed a few tears. When I first saw the state of his hooves, they reminded me of Aladdin's slippers. I think he knew straight away he was safe, as he let out a gentle although pathetic Eeyore. We had a deep straw bed waiting for him to try and help relieve some of the pressure to his poor hooves and within ten minutes Adam and our farrier arrived to help. Jason our farrier was disgusted and agreed this was total neglect and if the owners could be found they should most definitely be prosecuted under the Animal Health and Welfare Act 2013. Apparently, the act states you have a legal responsibility to your animals and any animals in your care. If you cannot or will not look after your animals, you should not have them. Honestly Ems, Jason was livid and so was Adam", Freya continues.

"Adam administered more pain relief and told us Snowy would need this for a number of weeks whilst Jason worked on treating his hooves which he said was going to be a very long job. Between us all we came up with a fabulous feeding programme that would benefit Snowy. We decided to keep Snowy isolated for the first two weeks and after this period, we started on a worming programme. Jason also advised us to soak Snowy's frogs every day for two weeks as they hadn't seen daylight in over two years. He said this would help his hooves get ready for the work he would need to carry out", Aunty explains.

"Do you know another thing Jason said?" butts in Freya.

For a slight moment I am unable to answer. How can an innocent little donkey be allowed to get into this state of neglect in the first place? I can feel my blood boiling. Animals do not have a voice. We need to be their voice.

Freya continues, "Jason asked Aunty and me to walk across the yard on our heels and then tell him how our legs felt. We tried it for a few paces and had to stop as the pressure and soreness we felt on our calves was unbelievable. It made us realise what pain poor Snowy had been in, having to walk like this for over two years", says Freya angrily.

I try as hard as I can, but I cannot stop that single tear that has been threatening.

"Jason managed to take off the worst of the curl to the hoof on day three. We gave Snowy extra strong painkillers beforehand and he really was a little star. Snowy had a seven-day break to give his hooves chance to recover and a week later Jason came back to continue to work on shaping them, followed by every week thereafter. Honestly Ems, it so nice to see his hooves looking more like they should be. He is still on a small amount of pain relief and Jason seemed very happy with his progress when he came to check on him yesterday", Aunty informs me.

"Snowy has slowly gained weight. When Adam comes tomorrow, if he is happy with his progress, we hope to be able to let him out for a stroll and a graze in his paddock. Fingers crossed", smiles Aunty.

"I was just thinking. Jess and Nicky are usually here on a Sunday. Why aren't they here today? I was so looking forward to hearing some more of their funny stories", I say to Aunty whilst gently stroking Snowy.

"Nicky's niece is getting christened today up in Derbyshire. Don't worry they will be here next weekend Ems", smiles Aunty.

I glance at my watch to see it is two o'clock already.

Chapter 6

✳ ✳ ✳

"WHAT ARE OUR PLANS FOR this week?" I ask Aunty.

"Well Ems, I thought we could try and go on a beach ride tomorrow after Adam has been. That is if you and Freya would like to of course?" she smiles back.

"Yes please", Freya and I excitedly call out at precisely the same time.

"As I have help, this week from Charlotte and Nick, I was thinking maybe you should use the mornings to do your assignments Ems. We could ride or do schooling in the afternoons, and you could type up your course work early in the evening whilst I prepare dinner. What do you think?" asks Aunty.

"That sounds a fabulous plan to me Aunty. I cannot wait to get cracking with Speckle", I grin.

"Come on, shall we go and get a snack? You can come out later to see the ponies properly", smiles Aunty.

I slowly get up and give Snowy a gentle kiss on his velvety muzzle. I am sure he is smiling at me.

"Can I give Snowy a groom later Aunty? He is such a cutie", I ask.

"Of course. I am sure he would thoroughly enjoy the extra attention", she replies.

After a quick sandwich followed by lots of chatting and giggling, we eventually head back out to the yard.

Freya and Aunty decide to do some more halter work with Shadow and Fern, so I head off armed with my grooming kit in the direction of Snowy.

As I slowly open the stable door, I have never heard a cuter Eeyore in the whole of my life.

"Hey Snowy. I am back. Would you like me to groom you?" I gently ask him as he looks directly up at me with those gorgeous almond eyes.

I chat merrily away to him as my body brush slowly caresses his beautiful white coat. Snowy's little head is high in the air, his splendid velvet muzzle moving from side to side in sheer delight. I smile to myself.

I think I am falling in love again.

I pick up my mane comb and gently groom his tail. I stand back and look at how splendid it looks. My plastic comb slowly runs through the soft white strands of his mane. He really is enjoying this pampering session.

Forty minutes later and I am thrilled with how bonny he looks. I turn to pack my grooming kit away when suddenly I hear the straw rustling. Can you believe Snowy is having a good old roll, with his little legs high in the air? This gives me the opportunity to have a quick glance at his hooves. They are so tiny, even smaller than the foal's hooves, and I am relieved to see, they seem to look more like the shape they should be.

"Hopefully you will be able to go out in the paddock tomorrow", I say to him as I plant a gentle kiss on his head.

"See you shortly", I call whilst shutting the door.

I immediately set off in a canter to find Aunty and Freya.

I am truly astonished to see how much Shadow and Fern have grown. Aunty is busy grooming Shadow whilst he stands patiently munching on his hay. How different he looks without all that fluffy foal hair. His striking bay summer coat is gleaming in the sunshine. He looks so grown up.

My mouth is wide open as I watch Freya groom Fern. His strawberry coat is glistening in the sun rays. He looks relaxed and calm. What has happened to the naughty little foal who didn't want to be caught and had fun bowling us all over.

"What do you reckon Ems?" grins Freya.

"He is a totally changed character. How did that happen?" I ask in astonishment.

"Freya has been working very hard with these two, spending regular quality time with them and just look at the results. Hasn't she done an amazing job Ems?" butts in Aunty.

"Wow. Well done Freya. What an achievement. I am so proud of you", I tell her.

Freya is grinning from ear to ear.

"I learned a lot from watching you and your body language with Speckle so decided to give it a try. It didn't work for me and Speckle, but I feel my magic has worked on these two", she grins.

"Absolutely", I reply as I walk over to give Fern and Shadow a hug.

"Val is doing a home visit on the family tomorrow who are interested in adopting both of our babies. They live around thirty miles away, have a cottage by the sea which is set in five acres of land. The Mum is very experienced and has two young children, one aged two and the other is only one year old. She works from home and together with her husband they share an ex-racehorse which they rescued seven years ago. They did all the retraining themselves. It all sounds very promising. The Mum who by the way is called Dee, feels Fern and Shadow would be the ideal pair for her children to ride, in around four years-time. Fingers crossed", smiles Aunty.

"How truly wonderful would that be for Fern and Shadow if it all works out? The two of them will be together forever", I reply happily.

"How was Snowy?" Freya asks me.

"That little guy is making me fall in love with him very quickly", I laugh.

"If Adam gives him the all clear tomorrow to go out into the paddock, I may put Shady and Benny in with him, so he has some company. What do you think?" Aunty asks us both.

"That is a brilliant idea Aunty. He must really be confused after what he has been through. I bet he is also missing his friend. I think it would help perk him up", I blurt out.

"I totally agree with Ems. When Shady and Benny go back to their home on Wednesday, we could always put Bella and Hope in with him to keep him company?" says Freya.

"What a great idea Freya. Ok let's turn these guys back out into the field as I cannot believe it is five o'clock already. I will then pop and turn Amber and Crystal out and we can get cracking on mucking their stables out and clearing the fields. We also need to muck out and feed Snowy", says Aunty.

"Mums not picking me up until six thirty so why don't Ems and I crack on with everything, as I am sure you have lots to do", says Freya.

"Oh, my word. Are you two sure? It is so lovely having us all together again. Thank you, my girls. I will walk the dogs and Tinker and get cracking on our dinner", smiles Aunty gratefully.

Off Freya and I go with our wheelbarrows. Thirty minutes later and the big field is clear. We get interrupted several times by Bella requiring my attention, and can you believe demanding a five-minute massage! We muck out Amber and Crystals stables in record time and trot over to give Snowy his dinner. I hold his food bucket whilst he gently eats his dinner. I must say it smells absolutely-delicious. There is most definitely garlic mixed in here somewhere. Freya picks up his droppings and removes the wet straw. She gently shakes up half a bale of fresh straw to add to his very deep and cosy bed.

We both blow him a goodnight kiss.

"See you tomorrow Snowy", I call to him.

Freya shouts her goodbyes before rushing off for her ride home. I make my way wearily back to the house. I have just realised how absolutely exhausted I feel. I am not surprised as I have been up since four am. To be honest, I can't wait to crawl into bed.

Aunty excels with dinner as always and after washing up the dishes I think she can see how tired I look.

"Ems if you want to have a bath and an early night, I completely understand as you have had a long day and look totally worn out", she says.

"Would you mind? I do feel completely shattered, I would love to have a soak in the bath, hopefully followed by a good night's sleep. I am sure it would do me the world of good", I respond.

"Ems. I am truly thrilled to have you staying here again and this time for three whole weeks. There is a local show jumping and gymkhana event just two miles away, next Sunday the tenth of August. I thought it might be fun for you and Freya to take Hope and Bella to?" says Aunty as she gives me a goodnight hug.

I suddenly feel wide awake again.

"Oh, yes please Aunty. That would be truly awesome", I smile.

"Sweet dreams, oh and Ems don't forget to shut your bedroom door", she laughs.

Eight thirty-five and my eyes will no longer stay open. I cannot believe Bella and I are not only going to the beach tomorrow, but we are also going to be competing in gymkhana games and show jumping soon too! My eyes feel so heavy.

Chapter 7

* * *

I MUST HAVE SLEPT LIKE a log. I cannot believe it is seven thirty in the morning. Opening my eyes, I look around and for a split second, wonder where I am.

I wash and dress in a flash.

"Good morning Ems", says Aunty in a very chirpy voice.

Tinker trots merrily towards me letting out a little bleat. I lean over and open my arms to give him a morning cuddle.

From out of nowhere all four dogs come flying towards me at great speed and before I know it, I am flat on the floor with wet tongues eagerly licking my face.

"Come on you lot, give Ems some peace. Let her have her coffee", smiles Aunty.

"Adam has just confirmed he will be here around eleven-thirty to check on Snowy. What are your plans this morning Ems?" asks Aunty.

"I need to do a two-hour slot with Speckle, and later I need to type my report with any progress made. Do you think it would be ok to turn Hope and Bella into the sand school so I can give Speckle my full attention?" I ask.

"What a sensible idea Ems. When you have had your breakfast, I will come out with you. Charlotte and Nick should be here just before nine to help me with the morning round, so you have plenty of time to spend with Speckle", she replies.

I must say Bella seemed a little miffed when I led her out from the field to the sand school although she immediately perked up as soon as Hope joined her. I watch with delight as the two of them canter around in the glorious sunshine.

"I will be back later. Please don't tire yourselves out. We are off on a fabulous ride to the beach this afternoon", I tell them.

They seem oblivious to anything apart from each other. Oh well, when Bella is happy, I am happy.

Armed with my bum bag full of pony nuts and a body brush, I make my make to the big field.

I can see Speckle over at the far end. This is what I had hoped for. Charlotte and Nick are busy poo picking with Aunty. I haven't met them yet, but it feels like I already know them as Aunty talks about them a lot.

Speckle lifts her beautiful head as I approach. A gentle little whinny escapes through her nostrils and a big smile emerges across my face.

"Good morning my gorgeous girlie", I say in a gentle voice.

Speckle is walking directly towards me. I stop in my tracks. She continues to come to me. Within seconds her tongue is slowly licking my right hand. I truly cannot believe this. As slowly as I can, I move my left hand into my bum bag to get some nuts as she continues to lick me.

She gently takes the nuts from my hand, I slowly move my right hand to her neck. She doesn't even flinch. I continue to tell her in a very soft voice how beautiful she is as my right hand gradually strokes her smooth silky coat from the top of her neck to the bottom.

"I think you are really enjoying me stroking you Specks, aren't you?"

"Oh, I am so sorry, I hope you don't mind me calling you Specks?" I ask.

She gently licks my hand, so I am assuming she is saying yes. *Phew!*

I continue to load my left hand with nuts and as casually as I can, retrieve the body brush out of my trouser pocket. Specks still hasn't resisted.

"Specks, my hand is going to feel different in a moment. It is going to feel soft and smooth against your skin. I promise you, you are going to love it. You trust me, don't you? You know I would never do anything to hurt you", I murmur.

I am sure she is enjoying me chatting to her as she has not moved an inch as I casually groom her neck with the body brush.

"See. How nice is that my girl?" I ask her.

She is still focussed on the nuts I am feeding her, so I gradually move the brush down to her chest.

"Good girlie. I am so proud of you. You continue to eat, and I will keep grooming you", I tell her.

I can feel how relaxed she is. I am totally thrilled. The body brush is gently gliding over her withers down to her back. No protest from her.

Wow, I didn't expect this.

I stop and turn with my head low and take four steps away from her. I can feel her close behind me. I stop. I can feel her warm breath blowing on my hand. I turn and with my right hand, gently stroke her neck. She doesn't seem bothered. I continue to talk to her as I lift my left hand to stroke her on the underneath of her neck. I move in closer. I lean my face into her soft, warm chest and as casually as I can, wrap my arms loosely around her. She doesn't move. I am last cuddling Specks. I would never have believed I could achieve this on day one. This is a very precious moment and I feel truly honoured.

I work hard concentrating on my breathing, keeping it slow and even. I want to stay this close to her forever.

I drop my arms, turn and walk another five strides away, my head hung low and I wait patiently.

Within seconds Specks is by my side.

Once again, I slowly move my hands to stroke her neck. I can see her eyes starting to close. She truly is enjoying every moment of this. My cheek is leaning against her neck. I move my arms until they are wrapped loosely around her. I feel truly connected as I think to myself this must be the closest a human has ever got to her without her being under sedation.

I stay as still as I can. I want to cherish every second of this huge step forward.

Whisper whinnies to Specks but Specks stays with me!

"It's ok baby. You can go and see Whisper if you want to. We have taken massive steps forward today. I am so proud of you", I tell her as I gently kiss her neck.

I release my arms and very reluctantly Specks starts to walk towards Whisper. She stops after ten strides, turns her head, looks straight at me and whinnies.

I have a lump in my throat and my lips are quivering. I am full of emotion and a tear threatens. I feel on cloud nine as I watch Whisper and Specks groom each other.

I cannot wait for our session tomorrow.

I glance at my watch. Eleven o'clock already. I canter to the sand school and within ten minutes Bella and Hope are back happily grazing in the field.

At last I have chance to say hello to Charlotte and Nick. I must say we hit it off famously as we sit on the deep straw beside Snowy waiting for Adam to arrive.

To cut a long story short, Adam gave Snowy the all clear to go out into the paddock. He will still need to remain on mild pain killers for now, but he hopes it won't be for too much longer.

Another memorable moment is when Aunty led Snowy out into the paddock. He walked very cautiously and a bit gingerly but after two years of not being able to walk without pain, this was a truly special moment. He let out a very pathetic Eeyore and received lots of whinnies back from the big field. After around ten minutes, he finally settled and put his head down to graze. I have absolutely fallen head over heels in love with him.

Aunty is going to put Benny and Shady in with him when we get back from our ride later. She is going to leave the two stables doors open so they can choose whether they want to stay in or out.

Chapter 8

* * *

WE HAVE A QUICK SNACK and by three o'clock, Freya, Aunty and I are finally on our way to the beach.

Aunty is taking us a different route today and our ponies are pumping with excitement.

"Come on Freya", I say in a very teasing manner.

"What do you mean?" queries Freya.

"You know. I want to know all about Jamie", I reply.

"Ok. Well to start with I met him at college. Oh Ems, he has a true love for horses and is a natural around them. He is intelligent, kind and has the most gorgeous blue eyes I have ever seen. He writes me little poems and leaves them hidden in my coursework for me to find. I never imagined I would ever meet someone as wonderful as him", Freya says dreamingly.

"Good for you Freya. Does he have his own horse? When am I going to get to meet him? Where does he live? What course is he taking?" I ask without stopping for a breath.

"Ems, I feel as though I am on Question Time", laughs Freya.

"Jamie is eighteen years old, one year above me. He is on his extended diploma level three of animal management with science. Jamie has a gorgeous mare called Jasmine who is 15.2hh and together they have won many cross countries competitions, show jumping classes and have excelled in dressage. He is very into animal welfare and your Aunty adores him. His dream is to work with abandoned horses, ponies and donkeys all over the world. Ems he is truly passionate about the welfare of any animal. That is why I love him", blurts out Freya.

"OMG, did I just hear right? You are actually in love with him", I tease.

"Oh Ems. It was just a figure of speech", Freya stutters, whilst blushing.

"We have only been seeing each other for seven weeks Ems, so very early days", she tries to justify.

"I am only teasing Freya. I hope I am going to get a chance to meet him. I need to make sure he is good enough for you", I smile.

"Come on Ems. I will race you down the track to catch up with Aunty", she replies obviously trying to change the subject!

I urge Bella into a trot but as usual she has other ideas. We fly down the track and within seconds we have caught Aunty up.

"I am taking you to the furthest beach I know", says Aunty.

"It is a very busy time of the year with the children being on school holidays and if we want to have a little canter, the beach needs to be empty", she continues.

I look around at the surrounding beauty. There is a lovely warm breeze and I am sure I am beginning to taste the saltiness in the air from the sea. The trees look so much different to how they did in April. They are now fully alive and completely covered with several different shades of green engraved onto their beautiful leaves.

I can see many butterflies dancing around the wild flowers. They are magical to watch. Their colours fascinate me as they sit effortlessly on the flowers, flapping their delicate wings. I never knew there were so many different types of butterfly until Aunty told me.

Isn't nature wonderful?

I am bought back out of my day dream by a busy little bee who is buzzing around my face. What a hard-working life they lead. They spend all their lives dashing around pollinating plants and I learnt at school that this plays a very important role in the production of the human and animal food chain. I recently read an article and was fascinated to learn they depend on pollen as a source of protein to give them energy.

In the far distance, I can hear the laughter of children who are most likely playing on the beach making sand castles.

We must be getting close now.

Fifteen minutes later and the ground beneath us starts to change.

We are here.

The sand rolls like a golden carpet until it entwines with the sea in the far distance. Bella's head is high in the air as she snorts and breathes in the wonderful sea air.

I turn to grin at Aunty and Freya.

"Come on my girls. Let's go and check to see if the coast is clear", laughs Aunty.

"When Freya and I came last week, we could not ride on the beach as the sand was too hot from the strong sun rays. We rode home through the cool, shady woods. Thankfully it isn't too hot today, the clouds keep covering the sun and the sea breeze is truly refreshing.", she continues.

I can feel Bella is very excited underneath me. She prances across the sand, lifting her knees high into the air. I gently pat her neck and ask her to walk nicely.

To our delight, the beach is completely deserted.

Aunty says it is a long walk from the nearest car park which is over a mile from here, so families tend not to come this far.

We smile at each other, as we walk towards the sea. Crystal is striding out beautifully.

How amazing is this?

Eventually we stop at the waters edge, watching the waves gently flow over the sand, then vanish leaving a frothy foam behind. I look out across the miles of sea, and for a moment feel slightly overwhelmed at this magical sight.

"Who wants a paddle?" asks Aunty smiling.

This time Bella doesn't even hesitate as she follows Crystal and Hope into the glorious blue and turquoise coloured sea. You cannot beat this feeling. I look in awe all around us and sigh in contentment. We are surrounded by the mysterious and charm like enchanting sea. I lower my right hand into the water. I swirl my fingers around in the warm ocean. Bella is pushing her muzzle up and down in the water, splashing and snorting, all at the same time.

I smile at my stunning girl.

"Isn't this truly breath taking and captivating?" I think to myself but literally say it out loud.

"This has to be my most favourite place in the whole wide world", claims Freya.

"I can totally understand why Freya. I feel as though I am in a magical dream when I am by the sea. The sound of the waves is so therapeutic, I love watching them entwine with each other, until they disappear into the far distance out of sight", I smile dreamily.

"Who would like a canter", pipes up Aunty.

"Time for me to beat you once again Freya", I laugh.

I know for sure Bella loves it here, she is picking her legs up beautifully. I am positive she is smiling at me as I stretch down to look at her.

My jodhpurs and boots are wet, but I don't care. It is time for me to thrash Freya's backside.

"Let's trot over to the far side", says Aunty pointing.

"Crystal and I will go first. You two can follow, we will then make a turn, and I will be the starter, making sure you are both in line. We don't want any cheating, do we?" smiles Aunty.

Bella is desperate to go, I struggle to keep her still. She really is fighting me. I can't wait to let her run free.

I look at Freya who is standing alongside me with a huge grin on her face.

Chapter 9

∗ ∗ ∗

"On your marks, get set, ready, go", calls Aunty.

I loosen my reins and urge Bella forward. We literally go from a standstill, to a canter and a full-blown gallop within a few seconds. The sea breeze is racing passed my cheeks as I sit as low as I can in the saddle. I feel like a jockey again. I glance down to see the sand flying rapidly off Bella's hooves. A massive grin covers my face. I literally cannot tell you how fast we are travelling. Bella has the speed of lightning, we are locked in our happy bubble and I never want this to end.

I can hear Bella blowing. I gather up my reins and ease her down to a trot. I am slightly out of breath too. Our exhilarating gallop has left me feeling on top of the world. I lean forward and give Bella a well-done kiss on her neck and now have a mouthful of sand!

"Well done my baby. Wasn't that just truly amazing?" I ask Bella in between trying to get my breath back and chomping on grains of sand.

"Wow, how fast did you two go? I had no chance of getting anywhere near you", says Freya as she slows Hope down to a walk.

"I know. I am sure Bella is getting faster and faster", I smile back.

"It looks like you four had great fun", says Aunty as she pulls up alongside us.

"What a turn of speed Bella has Ems. Well done, such a fabulous display to watch. Freya you and Hope looked like poetry in motion, absolutely beautiful", she continues.

Freya and I grin at each other. We love it when Aunty gives us compliments.

"How about we jump off, loosen their girths and lead them back to the bridleway?" asks Aunty.

"Great idea", I say as I jump off Bella into the soft sand beneath us.

"Do you know what?" I blurt out.

"I am going to take my boots and socks off as I have the urge to feel the golden sand running through my toes", I continue.

"I will join you", says Aunty and Freya at the same time.

Within seconds my boots and socks are off. I take a deep, relaxing breath as my toes feel their way through the soft, warm grains of sand. This is heavenly I think to myself as Bella and I make our way across the beach. Her hooves and my feet flick up the sand in unison as we go.

"Wasn't that fun", says Aunty as we reach the bridleway.

"I haven't done that since I was a kid", she continues with a huge smile across her face.

I brush the sand from my feet and pop my socks and boots back on.

It is five fifteen by the time we finish washing our ponies off and get them settled in the field.

What lovely news to hear, Charlotte and Nick have done all the chores, so all Aunty needs to do now is put Shady and Benny in with Snowy. Fingers crossed.

Freya gives us both a hug, says her goodbyes and heads off home. She's on babysitting duties this evening.

Aunty and I grab two head collars and make our way over to the big field. I take Benny and Aunty follows with Shady.

Specks is right down the far end of the field, so sadly I don't have chance to pop and see her.

"Eeyore, Eeyore", calls Snowy as we walk towards the paddock with his two new friends.

"Ems, if you let Benny off first, I will wait a couple of minutes before letting Shady go", says Aunty.

"Now you be a good boy with our Snowy", I whisper in his ear before taking off his head collar.

We didn't need to worry. Benny trots straight over to Snowy and immediately settles down next to him and starts to graze.

Aunty removes Shady's head collar and we watch closely as he trots over to Benny and Snowy, puts his head down and starts grazing too.

Aunty and I smile at each other. It looks like they have always been together. How sweet.

"Right Ems. I am going to hang around for a while just to be one hundred percent sure they are all ok. If you want to, why don't you nip and jump in the bath. I know you have your notes to type up too. I will get our dinner ready for seven o'clock?" says Aunty in a very chirpy manner.

"If you are sure, that would be great Aunty. I can't believe how fast today has gone. I have had a splendid day, and I can't wait to see what I can achieve with Specks tomorrow", I reply.

Nine thirty pm and I am tucked up in bed reading through my notes. I am truly proud of Specks. I smile and close my eyes as I run through todays' wonderful events.

Chapter 10

* * *

I MUST BE DREAMING, BUT I can't be. Surely this must be real?

Someone is vigorously shaking my arm.

"Ems. Wake up", says Aunty urgently.

I sit bolt upright in a flash.

"Ems. You need to get dressed as quick as you can. There has been a fire down at Jane Parsons' farm. We need to get there as soon as possible to bring some of her animals back here to safety", she continues.

Surely this is a dream?

"Come on Ems. Quickly as you can. I will meet you in the horse-box. Please hurry up", she urges me.

Within two minutes, my jeans, t-shirt and jumper are on and I race out to the front of the house as quickly as I can.

"The fire engine is on its way. Apparently, the fire started in the tack room and their dogs alerted them that something was wrong. Thankfully they managed to let all the animals out into a paddock far away from the fire. From what I remember the stables are timber so the fire could get out of control and spread. Joseph is also on his way with his trailer', Aunty tells me in a very serious manner.

I glance at my watch. Just gone five am. We are driving down that bumpy part of the road. I hang on tight as Aunty indicates left. Ahead I can see a building with grey smoke swirling and twirling up towards the sky.

We are here.

I can hear sirens in the far distance. We jump out and I immediately see Joseph busy loading four sheep and two goats onto his trailer. We need to move fast.

"Oh Pam. Thank you so much for coming so quickly. The fire engine should be here any minute. The fire has taken hold of the four timber stables. If you could take my four ponies with you, I would be eternally grateful. The noise of the fire engine is going to freak them out", says the lady in a very stressed manner, who I am assuming is Jane.

"Joseph. Could you come here quickly, we need your help?" Aunty shouts.

"I want everyone to grab a pony and lead them into my horsebox, so we can get out of here as quickly as we possibly can. Come on let's go", says Aunty.

All four of us rush over to the field where the ponies are patiently waiting by the gate.

Joseph puts a comforting arm on my shoulder.

"We can do this Ems", he tells me.

Thankfully, all four of the Dartmoor ponies are wearing head collars. We each grab a lead rope each off the wooden paddock fence and in we go. The ponies do not move. Maybe they are in shock. I can see the fire burning in the distance, the smoke soaring high up into the early morning sunrise.

What well behaved ponies. Within minutes we have them safely in the horsebox.

"Come on. Let's get them out of here before the fire engine arrives. See you back at ours Joseph. Phone me if we can be of any more help Jane", Aunty calls as she jumps into the driver's seat and turns on the engine.

I can hear the sirens getting closer and closer. We need to get out of here now.

At the end of the drive, Aunty indicates right. Joseph is following closely behind.

Just in the nick of time.

I can see through my wing mirror the fire engine has just literally turned right from the opposite direction towards Jane's. I seriously hope the fire team can get the fire under control quickly to limit any further damage.

How sad this is for the family.

"Right Ems. When we get back home, we need to take the four ponies to the sand school and put some hay nets up along the fencing. I will get Joseph to put the sheep and goats in the stable next to Snowy. Looks like we got there just in time. Good job, my girl", smiles Aunty as we enter through the black iron gates.

To be honest, I am still not completely sure this isn't all a dream. I pinch myself and I will tell you now, it hurts. This is most definitely real.

Aunty informs Joseph of our plan. The ponies are quiet and munching on the hay in the horsebox, so we decide to settle the sheep and goats first.

Thankfully Snowy, Shady and Benny are grazing out in the paddock, so I immediately rush over to shut the gate to the corral.

"We should be able to get them through the side gate Aunty. I have shut Snowy's stable door, so it should be easier to guide them into the spare stable", I call out.

I watch as Joseph reverses the trailer as far as he can get to the side gate.

Perfect parking. The ramp is down and ready. I watch in delight as four beautiful sheep, slowly make their way off the trailer and into the yard. I laugh at what happens next. The two goats come flying down the ramp, kicking out their back legs as they go with their heads held low and their horns ready for action. They come to an abrupt halt as the sheep baa at them.

Maybe they are telling them off. How funny.

"We need to get them into the stable", Aunty informs Joseph and me.

I rush to the far end of the corral. Snowy, Benny and Shady are standing at the gate watching the goings on with great interest. Aunty is standing at the other end and Joseph looks like he is going to have a go at being the Shepherd.

I slowly walk towards the goats and sheep. They shuffle around a little, but thankfully start to move forward towards the stable.

At this precise moment, Snowy decides to let out the loudest Eeyore I have ever heard him do. The two goats come heading towards me at full pelt. I immediately bend over with my arms over my head to protect myself. I can feel something jumping on my back and then nothing. I stay as still as a statue.

I can hear Joseph and Aunty laughing loudly.

"You can stand up straight now Ems", calls Aunty.

"We have them safely locked in the stable", she continues.

Joseph is heading towards me with that big cheeky grin on his face.

"Come here my beauty", he says before moving towards me. The next thing I know he has hold of me tight and is swinging me round and around.

"You certainly needed a Joseph hug, Ems", he grins.

At last my feet are safely on the ground.

"Good to see you too", I smile back whilst trying to regain my balance.

"Who was it who jumped on my back?" I ask the pair of them.

"It was one of the goats Ems, he used you like a trampoline. He or she then catapulted themselves off, jumped against the stable wall and thankfully followed his friends into the stable. It really was kind of funny Ems", laughs Joseph.

'I suppose it is', I think to myself.

"Well, they will be fine. They have a thick straw bed, some beautiful hay and plenty of water. Shall we go and sort the ponies out now?" asks Aunty.

I can hear her phone ringing loudly as we make our way towards the horsebox. I watch closely and although I can't hear what she is saying, she has a beautiful smile across her face.

Surely this is a good sign?

"Fabulous news from Jane. The fire crew have managed to put the fire out very quickly. Thankfully the fire damage was limited to the tack room and one stable. She wants her babies back so I have told her we will drop them back to her this evening. This will give her chance to get things sorted and contact the insurance company etc. Jane said they can all stay out in the fields. They were only in the stables due to the flies being a nuisance", Aunty informs us.

"That is wonderful news", I blurt out.

"I have to be in Cornwall by nine am, but I can make sure I'm back by six o'clock at the latest to give you a hand, if that isn't too late?" says Joseph.

"If you are really sure? That would be a great help, as it will save me doing two trips. Luckily, it doesn't get dark properly until nine o'clock, so we will have plenty of time to drop them back. Do you know what Joseph? I think you have just earned yourself another one of my famous fry ups", laughs Aunty.

Joseph has the biggest grin I have ever seen across his face. His beautiful white teeth gleam brightly in the early August sunshine. What is Freya going to say when she hears she's missed all this? Well she shouldn't be jealous, should she? She now has her own Joseph lookalike called Jamie?

Watch this space!

Aunty asks me to pop and get some hay nets ready and put some buckets of water in the sand school.

"The four ponies should be fine until we take them home this evening. Thankfully today is going to be cloudy and only twenty degrees, so they won't get too hot.", says Aunty as she walks back to her horsebox with Joseph.

Within ten minutes, the sand school is all ready for our temporary visitors.

I look up the yard to see Aunty and Joseph walking towards me with two ponies each. They really do look very well behaved and completely adorable. A lot of whinnying takes place but within ten minutes they all settle down and start munching quietly on their hay. I glance at my watch to see it is only six forty-five am. To be honest, it feels like it should be bed time.

We say our goodbyes to Joseph as he needs to be on his way. Aunty and I make our way to the house as we are in desperate need of a well-earned cup of coffee.

I cannot believe this just happened.

Chapter 11

∗ ∗ ∗

"GOOD MORNING EMS", I hear Aunty saying.

I slowly open my eyes.

What is going on? I am totally confused.

"Are you ok Ems?" asks Aunty as she places a mug of coffee onto my bedside cabinet.

I glance down at my watch to see it is seven thirty am. Impossible, that can't be right.

What am I doing in bed?

"What about Jane and the animals?" I blurt out.

"Who Is Jane?" queries Aunty.

"You know Aunty, Jane Parsons from the farm, down the road. The fire? We have her ponies, sheep and goats here", I reply.

"Ems, I don't know anyone called Jane Parsons. We certainly haven't got any extra ponies, sheep or goats here, certainly not when I checked half an hour ago", laughs Aunty.

"Aunty you really sure?" I ask, in a very shocked manner.

"One hundred percent sure Ems", Aunty reassures me.

"But it was so real Aunty. Joseph was there too. Her tack room and stables were on fire", I tell her.

"Ems, you must have been dreaming again", she smiles.

"I am going to walk the dogs and Tinker and you can tell me all about your dream over breakfast. It sounds very adventurous and exciting", she says as she disappears out of sight.

How bizarre is this? I still cannot believe it was only a dream.

Aunty is totally enthralled as I tell her every detail about my dream.

"Wow Ems. I have to say, that is a really exciting story", she beams once I have finished.

"I wish I could have adventurous dreams like you. I do dream, but I forget them as soon as I get out of bed", she laughs.

Nine am and it is me and Specks time.

We make truly amazing progress. This morning I decide to work more on touch techniques. I am over the moon when Specks allows me to stroke her ears and the front of her face. Another big step forward. I am one hundred percent convinced she is enjoying all the attention she is getting, and my plan for tomorrow is to get Specks used to having a head collar near to her.

How amazing would it be if I could get a head collar on her?

Freya and I have planned to meet Jamie and Jasmine at two o'clock. We are going for a ride around the stunning Devon countryside. I am looking forward to meeting him and his gorgeous mare. Aunty is staying here as Jet's new family are coming to pick him up at three o'clock. Fingers crossed for the gorgeous boy. I hope it all works out for him and that he will be very happy in his new home. I will of course keep you posted.

"Jamie and I are going to take you on a fabulous ride this afternoon Ems. We are going to ride to Berry Pomeroy Castle. It was abandoned in the seventeen century and many stories have been told about this haunted castle. Jamie knows a lot about the history as it was part of his history project at school", informs Freya, as we ride out through the black iron gates.

"Haunted? Really?" I question.

"Oh yes indeed Ems. One story is a about a lady who is dressed in white. I believe she haunts the dungeons and St. Margaret's Tower. Apparently, she was imprisoned by her very own sister as she was so much more beautiful than her. The lady in white spent years and years living in the dirty dungeons under the castle and eventually starved to death. Some people have even said they can feel her presence on the narrow stairs that lead down to the dungeon. Others have even felt her brush past them", continues Freya.

I can feel a shiver running down my spine.

"There they are", smiles Freya pointing over to the right.

I look over to see a stunning bay mare walking towards us. Bella and Hope whinny to Jasmine.

"Hi Jamie", says Freya in a very girlish way.

"Hi Freya. Ah you must be Emily. What a pleasure to meet you at last. I have heard so much about you, I feel I already know you", says Jamie with a big smile across his face.

I suppose I do have to admit he is kind of cute, although I am more focussed on Jasmine as she is truly breath taking.

"It is wonderful to meet you too Jamie", I smile back.

"I was just telling Ems about the lady in white, although I am not sure she believes me", grins Freya.

The country road we are walking down is surrounded by fields and outstanding scenery.

"It will take us about an hour to ride to the ruins. We can grab a cold drink at the castle before making our way back. It is tucked away in a deep wooded valley and I have ridden there many a time before", says Jamie.

"Do you really think it is haunted? I am not sure I want to go near it if it is", I respond.

"Ems. Don't be such a baby", laughs Freya.

"Emily. I can tell you many stories. There is also thought to be a child ghost called Isabella. Her fearful presence has been felt in the kitchens. She was the illegitimate daughter of one of the servants. One evening she walked into the kitchen to witness her mother being attacked by visiting noblemen. She rushed in to help her mother and sadly they were both killed. Such a sad story as Isabella is thought to have been only nine years old. Rumours say she is so desperate to seek help for her mother, and frequently follows visitor's home", says Jamie in a very sad way.

"No", I gasp out loud, making Bella jump.

"I am so sorry baby. I didn't mean to scare you. What a very sad story", I say.

"Are you sure it is completely safe to go there? I certainly don't want her following me home", I continue.

"Don't worry Emily, I have many more stories to tell you and once we arrive at the castle, you will be able to visualise it better then," laughs Jamie.

"Maybe we can change the subject for a while", I say as at last we turn onto a bridleway.

"Who fancies a canter?" asks Jamie without waiting for a response.

Jasmine glides across the ground ahead. Jasmine certainly has the action of a thoroughbred. I need to find out more about her.

Bella is taking a very strong hold. I try as hard as I can to ease her back, so she doesn't run up Hope's backside.

Even though it is August, I am grateful it hasn't been too hot. July's temperatures had soared to almost thirty degrees for nine days on the trot, so it had been impossible to ride.

I look ahead to see what looks like miles and miles of glorious woodland.

Chapter 12

* * *

"We will ride leisurely through the woods for around forty minutes, and then follow the gigantic trees as they slope deep down into the valley", smiles Jamie.

"Is Jasmine a thoroughbred?" I blurt out inquisitively.

"Correct. Spot on Emily. Jasmine is a well-bred horse and has an excellent pedigree. She was bred to race on the flat but after three races as a two-year old, each time finishing last, she was sent off to the sales. To be honest it is a very bizarre story how we ended up with her. At the time Mum ran her own horsebox company and had taken one of her clients to the sales. Mum had been sitting watching the horses go through the sales ring just minding her own business. Totally out of the blue, she had a terrible sneezing fit and as she went to stand up to get a tissue from her pocket, her right hand somehow went high into the air and the next thing she heard was, sold to the lady standing up for four hundred guineas", says Jamie.

"Honestly? OMG", I exclaim.

"Seriously Emily, Mum said she was totally shocked and didn't know how she was going to break the news to Dad. She didn't even know what she had bought but when she first saw Jasmine, her words were, 'This was meant to be'. She said she'd felt an instant love and connection with her, and she was sure my Nan was looking down and had made this happen. She said it was most definitely fate. Thankfully my Dad has a very wicked sense of humour and much to Mum's relief, he thought the whole thing was hilarious and happily welcomed Jasmine into our family. I was only eight at the time and ten years on, Mum and Dad are very proud of what we have both achieved", smiles Jamie whilst patting Jasmine very gently on her neck.

I can now understand why Freya has fallen for him. He has a kind heart and a fabulous sense of humour.

Good on Freya.

"Jamie. Why don't you just call me Ems, like all my friends do", I smile, as I look at Freya giving her the thumbs up.

Freya grins back, giving me the thumbs up too.

I smile as I listen to the birds singing their lullaby's as we ride through this truly stunning woodland. Flowers of all colours and shapes blossom under the sun rays which manage to sneak through the gaps in the trees. I watch as a striking grey squirrel runs quickly up a tree, a tiny rabbit grazes close by and butterflies dance merrily around.

"Look at what is ahead of us Ems", says Freya as she comes to a halt behind Jasmine.

I urge Bella forward. Down at the very bottom of the valley stands an enormous old ruin. It looks completely derelict. The stone work looks grey and worn. Green moss has taken hold over a large part of the building, the windows gape emptily and sadly the castle looks to have no life left in it. I can immediately see why this old neglected castle is said to be haunted.

I lean back in my saddle as we follow the track downwards through the woods.

We stand still in silence as we reach the end of the path. What I can see is truly breath taking. A very large area of beautiful green lawn rolls like a carpet directly up to the edge of the ruins. I look around in amazement. Trees which must be hundreds, maybe thousands of years old stand proudly all the way around the whole circumference of the remains. Their branches are covered in dark green leaves and some even spiral like sky scrapers, above the highest part of the castle.

"Three years ago, I came here on an audio tour as part of my coursework. As you walk around inside of the ruins, you get a feeling of it once being a very romantic and enchanting place", says Jamie glancing over at Freya whose cheeks are now glowing like those of a cooked lobster.

"Although in a couple of areas, especially the dungeon, I did feel my hair stand on end a few times", admits Jamie.

I shudder at the thought of the old cold and neglected dungeons and the horrible things that must have happened there.

"Apparently the castle was built by a very influential family in Devon called Pomeroy, hence the name. They sold it on in fifteen forty-seven to the Seymour family. Apart from a brief period when it was forfeited to the crown, it has always stayed in the same owner-ship. Jane Seymour became the third wife of Henry the eighth and was the mother of the only surviving male heir. Sadly, the castle was damaged by a lightning strike in the late seventeenth century and was abandoned due to the expense required to rebuild and the fam-ily moved on elsewhere. In the nineteenth century, poets and artists discovered this castle. The sheer beauty of the buildings and the sur-rounding woods finally inspired a revival of interest in the castle, and it became a tourist hot spot. It hosts regular tours and has a very popular and wonderful café", continues Jamie.

"Wow", I blurt out.

I have never really been into history but seeing this beautiful, although sad derelict castle in front of me, I now have the urge to know as much as possible about this enchanting place.

As we ride through the veil of trees and onto the path which leads directly to the castle, I have mixed emotions. I most definitely know one thing for sure. I would never, ever want to come here when it is dark.

"A smiling cavalier has been seen on the roadway outside the castle walls. It is said he has long black curly hair and an extra-large bushy moustache. People have claimed he has smiled at them and the ghostly cavalier has told them that he is on his way to the pub", claims Jamie.

I can hear echoing voices of tourists who must be inside the ruins and another cold shiver runs down my spine.

Right Freya, if you hold Jasmine for me, I will pop to the café and get us all a cold drink. This is about the nearest we can get to the castle on horseback, but we can ride around the perimeter later", says Jamie.

"What would you like to drink Ems", asks Freya as she takes hold of Jasmine's reins.

"If they have a seven up, that would be great. If not an orange juice please", I reply.

We watch as Jamie makes his way through the old castle ruins and disappears out of sight.

Bella has her head high in the air with her nostrils flaring. She suddenly starts to shuffle around whilst pawing at the ground. I gently pat her neck to calm her down.

"Don't be a silly girl Bella", I tell her softly.

"Apparently animals are very good at picking up on spirits", blurts out Freya.

"Do you think she has seen a ghost?" I reply, feeling slightly on edge.

"Jamie did tell me on one of his visit's here, how he'd watched a small dog who'd totally refused to enter the inside of the ruins. The dog had stood rigid, whilst staring directly ahead, growling fiercely in a very low and deep tone. With his heckles raised, he'd started barking as if he could see something or someone, but there was not a soul to be seen. His owners were very concerned as they had never seen him behave like this before. He wouldn't even take a treat from them", continues Freya.

Another shiver runs down my spine as Bella continues to fidget underneath me.

Chapter 13

* * *

We watch as Jamie emerges from out of the ruins, walking towards us with a big smile on his face.

"Here you go ladies", he says as he hands us both a drink and we thank him.

Within seconds he is back in the saddle giving Jasmine a pat on her neck.

"Come on, follow me and I will tell you a couple more stories whilst we walk around the outskirts of the ruins", he smiles.

Thankfully Bella feels more relaxed now we have started moving.

"Watch out for the ghost of the old gardener as we ride around the edge of the lawns. He has been seen by many visitors working away in the ruins scything the grass. A dog is also said to stalk the grounds of the castle. It is reported that when he is approached by strangers, he snarls and growls at them before fading away. Another ghost dog apparently resides in what used to be the great hall, and many tourists have attempted to pat him only to discover he has no substance", exclaims Jamie.

"No way", I say in a horrified manner, whilst another cold shiver quivers down my spine.

"You are just winding us up Jamie. In fact, I am starting to feel a little freaked out", I continue.

"Seriously Ems, I am not making this up. I will bring the book to you next time I visit, and you can read it for yourself", he replies in a very genuine manner.

"I promise I won't tell you any more ghost stories for now. I don't want to scare you Ems, although there are many, many more ghosts to be seen, including the guardsman, the cane bearer and the blue lady, to name but a few", he smiles.

"Don't be scared Ems. Ghosts would never hurt you", chuckles Freya.

"Freya don't be silly. I am not scared", I say in the most convincing manner I can muster.

"Freya, you go in front and I will stay at the back so I can protect Ems from the ghostly figures that haunt the old ruins", teases Jamie as he turns Jasmine around and takes his position behind us.

We chat as we walk around the outskirts of the ruins. I hadn't realised how big the grounds of the castle are. How different it must have looked in its glory days.

Bella comes to an abrupt halt. She is standing rigidly staring at something beyond the old cobbled wall at the rear of the castle. Her eyes are wide open, but I cannot see anything.

For a split second, something doesn't feel right. It is way too quiet and earie. Another cold shiver runs down my spine.

Without warning, the whole of Bella's body starts to shake as she lets out a very loud and powerful whinny which seems to echo for miles around. I certainly wasn't expecting this. To be honest I am feeling a little unnerved by it all.

Bella takes a few steps back whilst snorting in a very unusual manner. Another whinny bellows from her and I start to wonder if maybe she has seen a spirit.

"Surely it is time to start heading home?" I ask in a slightly shaky voice.

Freya and Jamie look at each other and laugh.

Freya and Hope start to walk ahead, and I follow closely, whilst trying to calm Bella down.

"Boo", shouts Jamie as he touches my left shoulder from behind.

I scream and nearly jump out of my saddle.

I can hear Jamie laughing loudly and my heart is going ten to the dozen.

"Ems. I am truly sorry for making you jump but I couldn't resist it. Please accept my apologies", he says, whilst trying very hard to contain his laughter.

I take a big deep breath and try to keep calm.

"Jamie, you are forgiven just this time but if you make me jump again, I am afraid you will have to go back to calling me Emily", I grin.

"Are you both ok? What was all that commotion about?" asks Freya.

I tell her what Jamie just did and she is laughing hysterically which sets Jamie off again. I can now see the funny side. The laughter becomes contagious and I can't help but join in too.

"Come on. Let's make our way home", says Freya.

It is gone five o'clock by the time Freya and I arrive back at Auntys.

Jamie had said his goodbyes earlier as he'd needed to head off home.

We will see him Sunday, as much to Freya's delight, he and Jasmine are coming to the horse show too.

We untack our ponies, give them a quick groom over, followed by a carrot and turn them out into their field. I am so relieved to see Bella behaving normally again. She really was freaked out by the goings on at the castle. We watch with a smile on our faces as they immediately canter over to their friends who are happily gazing at the far end of the field.

'I wonder how Jet got on?'

"Hey Ems, I am going to pop off home now. How do you fancy doing a bit of practice ready for the gymkhana in the sand school tomorrow, that is of course if it is ok with your Aunt?" asks Freya.

"Now that sounds a great plan, but don't you think we are a bit too old to be competing in gymkhanas? I will tell you Freya, I seriously never want to go anywhere ever again, where there is a possibility ghostly spirits could be hanging around. Do you understand? Never, ever, again.", I reply smiling.

"Don't worry Ems. I promise I will keep you away from any haunted castles in the future. By the way speak for yourself, I will never be too old to take part in gymkhana games", she laughs.

Chapter 14

* * *

As I make my way back towards the house, I notice Aunty in the paddock with Snowy, Shady and Ben.

I make my way across to the four of them.

"Hi Ems. How was your ride to the castle?" asks Aunty.

She laughs as I tell her the stories Jamie told me.

"To be honest, I have never visited the castle and after what you have just told me, I certainly won't be bothering", she laughs.

"How did it go with Jet this afternoon?" I ask her whilst I gentle massage Snowy's back and neck.

"Oh Ems, I am always sad when they first leave here to go off to their new homes. I am a silly old bat as I always end up shedding a few tears after they have gone", she sighs.

"That is understandable Aunty. You nurse your babies, and you teach them how to love and trust again after their terrible beginnings. You give them the chance to have a permanent loving home of their own and you should feel very, very proud", I reply.

"I know Ems and I will feel a lot better when they call me to let me know he is happy and has settled in ok. He was such a good boy and didn't even hesitate. In fact, he walked up the ramp and straight into the trailer like he'd done it many times before", smiles Aunty.

"He is such a lovely lad. You have done a wonderful job with him and I am sure he will be fine", I reassure her.

"I came out here to clear my head and give Shady and Benny a groom as their Mum and Dad are picking them up tomorrow morning at eight. Their flight from Australia landed an hour ago and they text me to say they cannot wait to see their babies again", Aunty tells me.

"They have been absolutely brilliant with our gorgeous little Snowy and I think it has done him the world of good having company", I reply.

"I totally agree Ems. If it is still ok with you, I would like to put Bella and Hope in with him when Shady and Benny have gone home?" she asks me.

"Of course, Aunty. I have a feeling Bella is going to fall head over heels in love with Snowy. He is so dinky, I bet he could even walk under her belly", I laugh.

"Oh Ems. It is so great having you here again. You really are a breath of fresh air. By the way, as it is your birthday on Friday, how about I treat you to a birthday meal at our local pub. They do cater for vegans", smiles Aunty.

"Oh yes please, I would love to. I seriously can't believe I am going to be seventeen. I can't wait to start taking driving lessons", I reply.

"You are growing up very fast, my girl", says Aunty.

"Is it ok if I go and type up my coursework? I need to do some research on what is going to be my next module. It is a tricky one as it is all about equine science", I tell her.

"Of course, Ems. Off you trot. Your jacket potatoes will be ready and waiting for you around quarter past seven. Happy studying", she says as I bend down to give Snowy a very big kiss on his little muzzle before heading back to the house.

Within an hour I have typed up the notes from my session with Speckle this morning and smile to myself with the progress we are making in such a short time.

The equine science module looks very interesting and I am delighted to see I already know about twenty percent of the course. The rest of it in some places looks very challenging but I will worry about that when I get to it.

After a lovely dinner, followed by the good news to say Jet has settled in well and has eaten all his dinner, I say my goodnights and retire to my bedroom. I cannot believe it is Wednesday already tomorrow.

Aunty has said it is fine for Freya and me to use the sand school and she has promised to dig out the show jumps she has stored in the barn and set them up so we can do some practice in preparation for Sunday.

Chapter 15

* * *

I OPEN MY EYES ONLY to realise I cannot move. A great weight is bearing down on my body.

'Oh dear', I think to myself as I suddenly remember getting up for a drink at two am. I must have forgotten to shut my bedroom door.

I try as hard as I can, to move my right leg. Absolutely impossible. Within seconds a lot of excited bodies are wriggling around on top of me and my face is being licked by several wet and happy tongues. I try to pull the duvet over my face, but it is too late.

"Morning Ems", says Aunty's cheerful voice.

"I thought I heard a lot of commotion going on", she laughs.

"Come on you lot. Poor Ems needs to get out of bed and have her breakfast before Shady and Benny's family arrive to take them home", she continues.

All four dogs obey Aunty immediately.

'Phew', I say to myself as one by one they leap off my bed and rush off to catch her up.

I jump out of bed as fast as I can and rush to close my bedroom door. I bend down to check under the bed just in case Tinker is waiting to jump out on me.

I walk to the bathroom and cautiously open the door. I don't trust Tinker and need to make sure he isn't hiding waiting to jump out on me like he has done before. No sign of him. *I wonder where he is?*

Eight-thirty am, and Aunty and I say our goodbyes as we wave Benny and Shady off. They really were pleased to see their family again.

I glance over to Snowy, who is now looking lonesome.

"Come on Ems. Shall we go and get Bella and Hope?" asks Aunty.

"Of course. I can't wait to see how they will all get on", I smile.

Off we trot to the big field, armed with our head collars and lead ropes.

'Eeyore', shouts Snowy in the distance.

"Morning my gorgeous girl", I say to Bella as I give her a big hug before putting on her head collar.

"I need you to be really nice to Snowy, Bella. He is such a lovely little lad and he could do with some tender loving care", I inform her.

I am sure Bella just winked at me.

Hope and Aunty follow closely behind us, as we make our way back to the corral.

'Eeyore', bellows Snowy as he lifts his gorgeous little head high into the air as Bella and I walk towards the paddock.

Bella and Hope whinny excitedly back to him.

I open the gate, double checking I have closed it securely behind me and we make our way across to Snowy. Bella gently lowers her head down towards the little donkey. Their muzzles eventually touch as they continue to smell and nuzzle each other. Bella tenderly licks one of his nostrils.

How sweet is that?

I turn to give Aunty the thumbs up with a big grin across my face. I remove Bella's head collar and Aunty leads Hope into the field.

Bella turns and walks over to meet Hope with her new friend Snowy following closely behind.

Snowy is walking so much better with each day that passes. I watch as Hope lowers her head to smell Snowy. Aunty removes her head collar and the three of them wander off and within seconds, have settled down to graze with Bella and Hope either side of Snowy.

Aunty and I look at each other and smile.

"Right Aunty. It is time for my session with Specks. Wish me luck", I say as I trot off to get my bum bag and a spare headcollar.

'Wow', I think to myself as I walk into the big field.

Whisper, Specks, the four foals and Juno have this all to themselves now.

Specks lets out a very soft and gentle sounding whinny and my heart instantly glows with love for her. I stand still and wait for her to come to me.

"Hello, my gorgeous girlie", I say to her as she gently licks my right hand. I have a head collar hanging over my left shoulder but thankfully she doesn't seem to be phased by it.

I reach into my bum bag for a handful of nuts and at that precise moment the head collar moves down my arm. Speckle takes a step back.

This is not what I wanted to happen.

"Come on Specks", I say holding the nuts out to her.

She gently takes them from the palm of my hand and moves a step towards me.

"There you go, that's better. I need you to get used to this head collar Specks. My mission is to be able to put it on you, attach a lead rope so the two of us can go and play in the sand school", I inform her.

She is looking at me in a very funny way.

She stands patiently whilst my right hand gently strokes her neck. As slowly as I can I move my hand down her back. Her little body feels warm and silky as I glide my hand back up to her neck. The head collar is still in my left hand and I hold it up for her to sniff.

"See. I told you it wasn't going to hurt you, didn't I Specks?" I tell her.

I move my right hand and gently caress her ears. My face leans against hers, I adore her smell and I am thrilled to say, she is absolutely loving this. I move my right hand around her throat area and back up to her ears. I want her to feel happy and relaxed with me stroking her around her head and ears.

I take two steps back and she follows me. She stops directly at my side. I turn and stroke her. I take two steps forward and stop. Here she is again, standing next to me. I stroke her and move on four steps this time and stop. She is right by my side.

I continue doing this on and off for around an hour. I am totally thrilled Specks chooses to spend time with me.

Today's session has been truly awesome. She is getting used to the head collar and I can touch her back with no problem at all. Tomorrow I will focus on getting her used to having her legs touched.

"I love you and I will see you later", I tell her as I give her one more gentle hug before making my way back to the house.

Chapter 16

* * *

I STOP IN DISBELIEF. BELLA is gently grooming Snowy on his rump. This is such a wonderful sight to see. Snowy is trying to groom Bella back although his neck is stretched out like a giraffe and he can only just reach her shoulder. I smile happily and quickly pull out my phone to take a photo.

"Hi Ems", Freya calls out to me.

"Quick Freya, come and look at these two", I call back to her as I point across to the paddock.

"OMG, that is the cutest thing I have ever seen", exclaims Freya.

"I was just coming to find you as your Aunty has popped over to the barn to get the jumps out. I told her we would see her over there to give her a hand. Would you rather practice jumping today or gymkhana?" Freya asks.

"Jumping", I reply without hesitation.

"Great. That's what I would prefer too", smiles Freya.

"Come on then, let's go", I reply as we canter off in the direction of the barn.

"Hello, my two girls", says Aunty who at this present moment is trying to move some old wrought iron hay racks out of the way.

We both rush over to help. I grab one end of the rack ready to lift it, when I realise, I have just put my hand straight through a very large cob web.

Immediately I scream and jump up and down in a completely crazy manner. I shake my hand furiously as I try to get the sticky broken web off me. The hay rack has accidently crash landed on Aunty's foot and she is hopping around shouting out in pain.

"Oh Aunty. I am so, so sorry. Are you ok?" I ask her in a very concerned manner.

"Don't worry Ems, I will be fine. Thankfully nothing feels broken", she reassures me.

"What was all that about Ems?" asks Freya.

"A gigantic cob web got stuck on my hand. There could have been a big black spider hiding inside waiting to get me. I don't like spiders", I reply, in utter disgust.

Freya is laughing so hard at the faces I am pulling.

"Well, well, well. Who would have known you had a spider phobia to go with your ghost phobia", she laughs loudly as she runs her fingers through my hair trying to mimic that of a crawling spider.

I yelp and jump back giggling.

Aunty joins in with the laughter, so thankfully she must be ok.

"Ems. I will warn you now. There could be a lot of spiders in here. It is a very old building and some of the stuff has been sitting here for over thirty odd years", says Aunty.

A shiver runs down my spine at the thought of how many hundreds, maybe even thousands of spiders that could be close to me at this precise moment.

"Why don't you leave me and Freya to sort out the jumps. You could nip back to the house and make the three of us a cup of coffee?" smiles Aunty.

I eagerly nod and gallop out of the spider barn and back to the house as fast as I possibly can.

Fifteen minutes later, armed with a tray carrying three coffees, I arrive back at the barn, only to find they are not there. I walk across to the sand school and see Aunty and Freya busy setting up six pairs of wings.

"Ems, could you do me a favour and drag some of the poles into the school?" asks Aunty pointing over to where they lay.

"We have left lots of hairy spiders on them just for you", grins Freya.

"Only kidding Ems. To be honest we didn't see any at all", she laughs.

Twenty minutes later, the jumps are all set up and our cups are empty.

Aunty has set up six single trotting poles, one three-foot jump, a double and a treble.

"Off you trot and get your ponies ready. I am going to spend some time with Snowy whilst you have some fun", smiles Aunty.

"Yes Ma'am, and thank you for your help", I tell her, whilst saluting her at the same time.

"Ditto Ma'am", pipes up Freya.

Forty minutes later and we are ready for our jumping practice. We walk and trot for fifteen minutes to warm them up and loosen up their muscles. Both have been eagerly eyeing up the jumps.

Chapter 17

*** * ****

"You go first", calls Freya.

"Come on baby. Let's get this show on the road", I say excitedly to Bella.

I encourage her forward and she immediately responds trotting fluently over the ground poles. We turn the corner and I gently ask her to canter. She is taking a very strong hold and we literally fly over the first jump. I try as hard as I can to bring her back as we turn to towards the double. I have no choice, but to trust Bella. She has got hold of the bit firmly in her mouth and there is nothing I can do apart from retain my jumping position. We fly over the double effortlessly as though she has wings.

"Easy Bella", I tell her.

I try hard to steady her as we turn towards the treble.

I am totally convinced Bella does not know what the word easy means. Once again, she takes complete control, jumps the first two of the treble beautifully, but is too keen and knocks the pole off with her hind leg on the third.

We continue to canter around the outside of the school whilst I try as hard as I can to pull her up. Finally, I regain control.

"Wowzee", says Freya.

"Talk about keen Ems. Bella was absolutely loving it", says Freya as I eventually pull up next to her.

"Tell me about it. Bella is so strong when she gets excited Freya", I reply.

I jump off Bella and hand her reins to Freya. I put back the pole we knocked off a moment ago and return to remount my baby.

Bella and I watch with delight as Freya and Hope make their way elegantly over the trotting poles. In a perfect collected canter, they clear the first jump, now for the double. Hope clears both by at least a foot and does the same at the treble. Freya is grinning proudly as she eases Hope to a walk, finally stopping next to me and Bella.

"Freya, that was a truly awesome display, you both looked absolutely fabulous out there and in complete control", I grin.

"Thanks Ems. I was thinking why don't we do some more flat work before you try the jumps again? We could do some circle and transition work? It may help settle Bella down a bit", suggests Freya.

After twenty minutes, Bella and I attempt the jumps again. This time I have total control and we clear them with ease.

Freya is grinning.

"So much better Ems, in fact that was truly awesome. I hope we are not going to be in the same class on Sunday as I think you will thrash my ass", laughs Freya.

"I need to remember to get the excess energy out of Bella before I jump her. Thanks for the advice Freya. Bella and I will be look forward to taking you and Hope on", I grin back.

'Eeyore', we hear in the distance.

Bella has her head high and her body starts to quiver as she whinnies loudly back to Snowy.

"That is so sweet Bella. You love our little Snowy, don't you?" I ask her with a huge smile on my face.

"He certainly is the most gorgeous little donkey I have ever met. I absolutely adore his ears and cute velvet muzzle", says Freya.

"Come on. Let's get Bella and Hope untacked and put them back in with Snowy", I say as I dismount.

I glance at my watch to see it is only four o'clock.

"Freya if you are free for a couple of hours, I would be happy to run through my notes on equine health and welfare with you?" I ask her.

"Oh Ems. That would be fantastic. I need all the help I can get", she smiles gratefully back at me.

I walk Bella around to the corral.

'Eeyore', shouts Snowy.

"Once again Bella whinnies back to him. I remove her head collar, and she immediately trots over to her new friend and instantly lowers her head to nuzzle him.

'So sweet. Maybe Snowy could be Bella's brother? I am positive Mum and Dad would definitely fall in love with him and Suki would too', I think to myself.

"How did you get on with your jumping?" asks Aunty as we walk into the kitchen.

"Really well in the end. Bella was rushing the jumps, so Freya suggested I did more ground work to settle her down and that worked a treat", I tell her.

"Well done Freya", grins Aunty.

"Have you been busy Aunty?" I ask.

"Yes. I spent some quality time with Snowy. My what a little treasure he is. I also received another update on Jet to say how well he has settled. So much so, she said it is like he has been there forever. Bev has sent me the completed home visit for Shadow and Fern. She has given the family a five-star rating and the photos of their home look truly amazing. They are coming to meet our two boys on Sunday, so fingers and toes crossed", smiles Aunty.

"How fabulous.", I reply.

Freya and I make our way into Aunty's office and I boot up my lap top. We get stuck in and two hours fly by as we discuss different topics throughout Freya's coursework. I have to say she was really focussed, and her confidence grew and grew. By the time we had finished, she said she was feeling much more positive and had a greater knowledge and understanding on equine welfare.

It is ten past six before she heads off home armed with her notes. I quickly type up Specks session and by seven o'clock Aunty and I are happily chatting whilst eating our dinner.

Nine thirty pm, after a long hot soak, I am last in bed ready to do some revision. By eleven pm, my eyes are feeling very heavy. I cannot keep them open any longer.

Chapter 18

* * *

I AM SURE I'VE SPENT the whole night dreaming once again. This time Bella and I were somehow in Ireland competing in a very prestigious cross-country event. I honestly haven't a clue how we got there. Did we fly? Did we catch the ferry? I try hard to remember but I can't. From what I could see, Ireland looks truly magical. The scenery was absolutely breath taking. Golden sandy beaches ran along the edge of the shore for miles, magnificent mountains stood boldly looking out to sea and acres and acres of green fields sat proudly all around.

Bella and I gallop towards the fourth jump. It is a solid, four-foot high obstacle constructed out of dark brown logs. We approach the fence, I urge her on and Bella soars over with inches to spare.

I am awake and back in my bed.

'How blooming annoying. I seriously cannot believe that was just another dream. It seemed so real and we were having so much fun', I mumble to myself.

"Morning Ems. I hope you slept well", greets Aunty.

I walk into the kitchen to receive my morning greetings from all four dogs and Tinker.

"I had the most awesome dream Aunty. Bella and I were competing in a fabulous cross-country event in Ireland", I smile.

"How wonderful Ems. I have been to Ireland many a time with your Uncle. It is a truly beautiful place to visit. I have very fond memories of my time spent there", smiles Aunty.

"I was thinking. How do you fancy a ride through the woods this afternoon? About two miles from here lies a beautiful country estate which is set in two hundred acres of land. It really is something you must see", she continues.

"Oh yes. That would be fabulous, it sounds lovely", I reply.

"I know Freya is coming over about one o'clock to help me do more work with Shadow and Fern. I thought tomorrow we could have an early lunch around one o'clock at the pub, followed by a ride to the beach later in the afternoon with it being your special birth-day", says Aunty.

"Aunty. I would love that. Thank you so much", I reply as a massive grin appears on my face.

"Time for me to go and work with Specks. See you later", I call as I make my way out the front door.

Bella lifts her head up and whinnies gently as she walks towards me.

'Eeyore', calls Snowy as he closely follows Bella.

"Good morning my babies. How are you today?" I ask, as I give them both a morning kiss. Within seconds Hope has joined us and all three demand my attention at the same time. *I need more hands!*

Armed with the head collar, body brush and not forgetting my essential bum bag which is full to bursting with nuts, I make my way over to the big field.

I can see Specks at the far-right hand side, close to one of the field shelters.

I slowly make my way towards her, but I am being followed by all four foals. I divert their attention by scattering some nuts onto the grass. This will keep them occupied for a while.

I am around twenty feet from Specks when she suddenly sees me. She whinnies and immediately starts walking towards me.

"Morning my gorgeous girlie", I say to her as she appears at my side.

I hold some nuts in my left hand. She gently takes them, as I slowly move my right hand to stroke her neck and head. She hasn't moved at all.

"Specks today we are going to be doing some more grooming. I want to be able to stroke your front legs and work towards your tail. How wonderful would it be to have a nice silky tail with no knots in it?" I babble away to her.

She is gently licking my left hand as I stroke her neck once again. I casually run my right hand tenderly down her shoulder.

"Good girlie", I tell her as I pull out a few more nuts.

My right hand continues to stroke her shoulder, then gradually moves around to the front of her chest. She is relaxed and thoroughly enjoying every second. My hand casually moves to the top of her near fore leg. I feel a little shiver underneath her skin.

"Did that tickle you baby?" I ask in a soft warm voice.

More nuts are ready in my left hand. My right hand moves as softly as it can in a gentle motion down to her knee.

"Good girlie", I tell her.

I pull out the body brush from my pocket and gently let the soft bristles flow over her neck and back. My left hand is offering her nuts. She is calm and relaxed. I stretch slightly to groom her rump. No reaction. The brush glides back to her chest and as slowly as possible down to her knee. She licks my hand. I swap the brush for my hand and tenderly run my fingers down to her hoof. I keep my breathing relaxed and steady. Back up to her chest I go and finish with both of my arms wrapped around her neck, my face against her soft warm skin. I cannot tell you how wonderful this feels. I want to stay here for ever, but I know I can't.

I slowly release my arms and invite Specks to follow me. I walk six paces and patiently wait until she is by my side. This time I have the head collar looped through my left hand. She reaches for the nuts and her muzzle touches the head collar and she doesn't react at all.

"What a good girl you are Speckle", I tell her.

"I am so proud of you", I continue.

I try once more. This time as she drops her head to take the nuts, her muzzle goes through the noseband of the head collar. I want to jump up and down in delight but stay as calm as I can. This is another massive step forward.

I drop the head collar gently onto the floor and put my arms around her.

"Specks, you have been an absolute star today. Tomorrow is my seventeenth birthday. What can we achieve do you think?" I ask her.

She lets out a gently whinny as if she is talking to me.

"I have to go now darling. I will see you later", I tell her gently planting a kiss on her forehead.

I know she is following me as I make my way towards the gate. We have another special moment when our eyes connect for quite a few seconds. I smile with love and delight.

Chapter 19

∗ ∗ ∗

THE SKY IS FULL OF fluffy white clouds as Freya and I follow Aunty and Crystal across the beautiful Devon countryside.

Rich green fields to my right roll for miles and miles, disappearing far away into the distance. To my left lie golden fields of harvested straw waiting to be baled up by the local farmer.

I absolutely adore this time of the year. I love to see wild flowers in full bloom sitting proudly amongst the grass verges, birds singing sweetly and of course the icing on the cake is, it is my birthday tomorrow.

We continue to ride down the country lane. It is peaceful with not a soul to be seen.

"I'm going to tell you both a story. In November last year, I was riding down this exact spot when I came across a lady who was shouting to me, whilst frantically waving her arms to get my attention from that field over there", points Aunty.

"As I rode towards her, I could she was standing next to a Smart car which sat lonesome in the field and a good thirty feet away from the road. She told me she had swerved to the right to miss a fox, had driven up the grass verge and straight into the field. Look, you can see where the field slopes downwards. We'd had quite a few days of constant rain, so the fields were wet and very muddy. Her car had started sliding down the field and she hadn't been able to get it back under control and it had continued to free-wheel down the muddy field. Eventually after slamming on the brakes and putting her hand-brake on at the same, although she skidded, the car finally came to a stand-still. She'd tried everything she could think of for about an hour to get her car moving but sadly to no avail. The wheels were coated in thick wet mud and she was well and truly stuck. Poor lady was shaken up to say the least but also very annoyed and angry at herself that she'd left her mobile phone at home", continues Aunty.

"What happened next?" I ask curiously.

"I immediately called Joseph who came to the rescue like a knight in shining armour in his Land Rover. He attached a tow rope onto the bolt at the back of the Smart car. The lady named Jackie was worried and not over keen to get back into her car. She held onto Amber and into the driver seat I jumped. Being an automatic car, Joseph asked me to put it into neutral and told me all I had to do was to sit still and steer. Well can you believe Joseph's four by four started kicking out tons of mud which covered my windscreen. He'd then started skidding and so did I. It was truly nerve wracking, I will tell you that for sure. Honestly it felt as though we were skating on an ice rink", says Aunty.

"Blimey, that does sound scary", pipes out Freya.

"What happened next?" I urge Aunty.

"Well, can you believe we then had Joseph's four by four and the Smart car both completely stuck? All eight tyres were covered in wet, thick mud and Joseph said only a tractor would have the power to pull both cars out", she continues.

"We tried calling Mr Jacob, who has the farm over there, but typically there was no answer", she says pointing over to the left.

"By now it was getting very cold and I decided it would be quicker to ride Amber to the farm so we could get help as quickly as possible. Eventually I managed to track down Mr Jacob who was tending to his cows and explained what had happened. To my relief, he said he would gladly help and off he went to get his tractor", says Aunty.

"Wow, this sounds like a right old adventure you had Aunty", I say.

"It certainly was Ems. Mr Jacob followed me to where both cars were stuck and within minutes the solid monster like wheels on the tractor fiercely ploughed their way through the field. Jackie and I had watched in amazement as the tractor started to pull Joseph's four by four backwards out of the field. I held my breath as Joseph's car started to skid to the left and then to the right as the tractor slowly dragged it towards us. Five minutes later and Joseph and his four by four were safely back on the road", Aunty continues.

"What about the Smart car?" asks Freya.

"Well I must say this was quite a hair-raising experience. Joseph was far too tall to sit in the driver's seat, Jackie didn't feel brave enough, so I had no choice, I had to be the driver. I watched through the driver's side mirror as the car started to glide and swerve to the left. It was such a bizarre feeling to be going backwards in a car I had no control over, as it slipped and glided underneath me. I'd tried as hard as I could to keep the steering wheel straight and I can't tell you how relieved I was when we eventually got back on the road", continues Aunty.

"Wow, well done you Aunty. It was lucky for Jackie you were riding by as she could have been stuck out there for hours. That would have been awful to have been marooned all alone in a cold muddy field with no phone", I tell her.

"You are right Ems. Jackie said she'd learnt a very harsh lesson and would never, ever go anywhere without her phone again", smiles Aunty.

"I would never dream of going out without my phone", says Freya.

"Me neither", I respond.

"That was a wonderful story, wasn't it my baby?" I say to Bella as I gently stroke her neck.

Aunty turns off to the left and we cheerfully follow the bridleway signs.

"We can ride around the outside of the Estate, we can't go all the way around, as we haven't got time. I just want to show you how beautiful it is. There are a few places where we can have a canter too", smiles Aunty.

Aunty jumps off Crystal to open a twelve-foot wooden gate. We follow her through as she shuts the gate and remounts Crystal.

I look around in sheer amazement. What a truly stunning view. In the distance I can see a magnificent white building, in fact it reminds me of the President's White House in the United States.

"Can you believe the main house has thirty-six bedrooms plus eighteen bathrooms and apparently all the sink and bath taps are solid gold throughout", Aunty informs us.

"Wow, really? Blimey, how long would it take to clean that house?" I say shaking my head at the thought of it.

"Who could ever use eighteen bathrooms?" says Freya in a very shocked manner.

"Come on my girls, when we get around the bend, we can have a canter, so get yourselves ready", smiles Aunty.

Bella takes a strong hold and immediately attempts to trot.

"No, you don't", I tell her as I gently ease her back to a walk.

My clever pony understands so many words, that is when she wants to!

Maybe we need to start spelling out the word canter, letter by letter like people do with their dogs who get over excited whenever they hear the word walk.

Chapter 20

✳ ✳ ✳

AUNTY HAS SHOT OFF AHEAD and within seconds we soon make ground up and are closely behind her.

Bella feels relaxed beneath me as I take a moment to glance around in awe at this idyllic estate. I cannot believe how many fabulous rides there are here in Devon.

Aunty slowly pulls Crystal up and Freya and I follow suit.

"This is what I wanted you to see my girls. Two fields from here you will see the most amazing sight ever. Just you wait and see", smiles Aunty.

Freya and I look at each other in a questioning way.

I wonder what we will see?

"Look", whispers Aunty.

My head turns, and for a moment I cannot believe my eyes. A stunning herd of deer are grazing happily in the enormous field which I assume must be their home. We stand still and watch in silence as we take in this wonderful moment.

"Aunty look", I say excitedly as I point to the far right.

A majestic stag is stood with his head proudly in the air. He has the biggest antlers I have ever seen in my life.

"Aren't they just an incredible species?" says Aunty.

"Did you know a stag, which is obviously the male, sheds his antlers in early Spring? A new set immediately starts to form which takes approximately sixteen weeks to regrow. Apparently, they are made of a dense and solid bone. My dogs absolutely adore chomping on their antlers, and they are good for cleaning their teeth too", says Aunty.

"Wow. I didn't know that. I can't see any babies", I say in a disappointed manner.

"Well, the fawns are always born in around May or June Ems so there should be some young ones out there somewhere. From what I can remember, I think they mate in October and November, and carry their babies for around eight months. The stags use their antlers to fight each other for the females during mating season", Aunty informs us.

A crow screeches loudly from a nearby tree.

At that exact moment, the herd of deer put their heads high into the air, spin around, gallop quickly away down the field and within seconds they are completely out of sight. The stag follows closely behind.

"Wow, how truly awesome was that to see?" I gasp.

"Come on my girls, there are a few more areas I want to show you", says Aunty in an excited manner.

Aunty jumps off Crystal once again to open another large wooden gate. We follow her through, wondering where we are going.

The path we are on is shaded by an avenue of magnificent looking trees. Their thick, solid branches reach high into the sky, eventually entwining as they meet. It seems as if we are under a roof, as it feels cooler and is darker as the trees shut out the sunlight.

"Listen", says Aunty.

"Can you hear that?" she continues.

We stand still. I can hear what sounds like water splashing nearby.

"Look to your left", says Aunty.

I turn to see a truly beautiful lake which has appeared from literally out of nowhere. I can see what I am sure are two white swans playing around in the water.

"Come on, follow me. We can get a little closer", Aunty says.

We saunter down the path and out into the open. It suddenly feels as though the roof has been lifted, the air feels warmer and full daylight has returned.

I have to say this is the most picturesque and mesmerising place I have ever visited. The ripples in the lake glisten in the sunshine. Trees in full bloom, covered in many vibrant colours surround the perimeter, their reflections seemingly mirrored onto the top of the water. I can see ducks floating around, quacking away to their hearts content. I smile. This is truly magical.

I urge Bella forward to the edge. Our reflection is imprinted on the top of the water just like the trees.

"Look Freya. How cool is this? There are now two of me and two of Bella", I laugh.

Aunty and Freya ride up either side of Bella.

"Now there are twelve of us", grins Aunty.

We slowly and carefully ride around the edge of the lake.

"Look over here", I say excitedly.

"Can you see all the different coloured fish swimming under the water? One just popped his head out and smiled at me", I grin.

"I would say that has to be a carp. The colourful one looks like a rainbow trout and I haven't a clue what the others could be", smiles Aunty.

I can smell the strong aroma from the masses of beautiful wild flowers carpeting the ground. I look closer into the lake. I see dragonflies darting around like the speed of light, twisting and changing directions just above the water.

"I wonder how many different animals, birds, and fish live on this Estate?" I ask.

"I wouldn't have a clue", answers Freya.

"Maybe I will google it later as I am intrigued", I reply.

"Sorry my girls, but we need to make our way back home now", says Aunty.

"This really has been such a beautiful ride Aunty. A hundred times better than that haunted castle", I reply whilst smiling sarcastically across at Freya.

The ride home was wonderful. We had a couple of fabulous canters. I nearly fell off when a branch hit me harshly across my right cheek when I was least expecting it. Thankfully I had been quick enough to grab a handful of Bella's beautiful mane and with some twisting and shuffling around, I'd managed to pull myself back safely into the saddle.

Snowy was elated to see Bella and Hope and for the first time ever, he managed to trot a couple of paces towards us as we approached.

How amazing was that?

I am thrilled to see Snowy looking so happy. He is obviously in less pain and has settled in perfectly.

Freya is on babysitting duties again and has rushed off home.

Charlotte and Nick left at three o'clock as they had a dentist appointment, so now Aunty and I are on evening duties.

Chapter 21

∗ ∗ ∗

I AM STILL ON A high after our awesome ride to the estate today. I canter off armed with my wheel barrow and pooper scooper and make a start on clearing the dung from the big field.

Shadow and Fern look to be playing ring a ring of roses. I stand and watch with a big smile on my face. It is going to be truly marvellous if the two of them can stay together. Fingers crossed for Sunday when they meet their prospective new family.

Juno is happy grazing alongside Misty and Trixy. Specks and Whisper are resting under the shade of the big leafy trees.

I have managed to collect nineteen poo's safely in the barrow. I should just about be able to fit in the last one.

'Phew, all done', I say to myself as I look around in satisfaction at the now pristine field, completely free of horse poo.

I make my way over to say goodnight to Whisper and Specks.

The pair of them look so relaxed and I smile as Specks' cute little nostrils scrunch up as I approach.

"Hey, my baby girl. You look so chilled standing there in the shade", I tell her.

I am disappointed not to be wearing my bum bag although Speckle doesn't seem to mind the fact, I haven't got any nuts with me.

She gently sniffs my hair and licks my left hand. I slowly stroke her cool, silky neck and slowly wrap my arms around her and hold her tight. She lets out a contented sigh as her beautiful heads sits quietly over my left shoulder. Another amazing moment for me and Specks.

'Bang', I suddenly jump at the unexpected noise, Specks takes a step back.

I look over to where I'd left my wheel barrow sitting. I am horrified to see it has been overturned. Shadow and Fern are having great fun pawing the dung which is now being spread over the field in all different directions.

"Specks. Can you believe that? They really are like naughty children, aren't they?" I sigh as I make my way over to reload my barrow.

"Are you sorry?" I ask the pair of them.

They take no notice of me as they are too busy having fun.

Eventually Shadow stops and looks at me with a very mischievous look on his face.

"Come here you little monkey", I say to him as I stroke him gently down his neck.

"How could I ever be annoyed with you?" I ask him.

Shadow jumps backwards and whinnies across to Fern. I am gobsmacked to see Fern galloping around the field with my poop scooper proudly hanging from his mouth.

I cannot believe how naughty the pair of them are.

Within a split-second Shadow is in hot pursuit of Fern who now has thankfully dropped my poop scooper. Trixy and Misty have also decided to join in the chase. I smile as Juno lifts his head, looks around and immediately settles back down to graze. I am sure he is tutting at the foals and their naughty antics.

Fern seriously has the speed of lightning, the other three have no chance and fail miserably to take the lead. Eventually they settle back down, and I get cracking on filling up my barrow once again.

On my way back to the house, I pop by to give Bella, Hope and Snowy a hug. I tell them what the cheeky foals had just been up to and as I get to the part about Fern running off with my poop scooper, Snowy let's out a very loud Eeyore and puts his gorgeous little head in the air, curling up his top lip at the same time. I am positive he is laughing at my story.

'*What a very cute and intelligent boy you are*', I think to myself as I giggle at the thought of him laughing.

I type up my notes from this morning and decide to give Mum a call. She said she is really missing me and Bella. I told her I will give her a call in the morning.

After a long soak in the bath, and a fabulous dinner once again made by Aunty, I head off to bed to carry on studying. I cannot believe I will be seventeen tomorrow.

Chapter 22

* * *

"WAKEY, WAKEY BIRTHDAY GIRL", I hear Aunty saying.

I stretch my arms high and open my eyes to see Aunty looking at me with a big grin on her face.

"I have brought you a birthday cup of coffee to drink in bed. I know you said you were going to give your Mum and Dad a quick call before your Dad heads off to works", she smiles.

"Thank you, Aunty", I smile as I glance at my watch to see it has just gone five past seven.

"I have a card and present in the kitchen waiting for you when you are ready. I know you have a card and present from your parents in your suitcase too, along with a few more, so don't forget to bring them all out with you", says Aunty as she disappears out of sight.

'Ring, ring'.

"Hi Mum", I say as I hear her chirpy voice.

"Happy Birthday love. I cannot believe my little girl is seventeen today. It seems impossible", says Mum.

"I can't believe it either", I laugh back.

"I am just going to pass you over to Dad before he heads off to work love. I'll speak to you in a moment", she continues.

"Happy birthday to my very special and grown-up girl", says Dad in a very happy voice.

"Aw, thanks Dad. It is so lovely to hear your voice", I reply warmly.

"Emily, I hope you have a fabulous day. I can't believe this is the first year we won't be with you to celebrate your birthday", he responds in a seemingly sad voice.

"I know Dad, I am going to miss seeing, you, Mum and Suki too. Shall we skype tonight when you get home from work?" I ask.

"That's a great idea love as I am just about to dash off now, so I will pass you back to your Mum and I will speak to you this evening. Have a fabulous day. Love you", he says.

After saying my goodbye's to Mum, I quickly check my phone as it has been beeping like crazy. I have fifteen birthday messages from friends and family, plus seventy-two notifications on my Facebook timeline.

'Wow', I think to myself as I quickly get washed and dressed.

I grab the carrier bag from my suitcase and rush towards the kitchen and place it onto the centre of the table.

"Aunty, can I just pop out and have five minutes with Bella?" I ask her.

"Of course, you can my girl. I will make you another cup of coffee for when you get back", she replies.

I am greeted by the sound of Bella's beautiful whinny followed by an Eeyore from Snowy as I make my way across to the paddock.

I wrap my arms around Bella and hug her tight.

"It is my birthday today Bella. Can you believe two years ago today you came to live with me? Look at the adventures we have been on together", I say with a big grin on my face.

"Ems", calls Aunty as I turn to see her trotting towards us.

"I found this present and card in the carrier bag. It is from Bella by the looks of it", she grins.

"My baby girl, you didn't forget", I tell her, as I hug her even tighter.

Aunty hands me the present which has a card sellotaped to the top.

It feels quite squishy.

I wonder what it could be?

I pull the envelope from the present and open the card to see one of my favourite photos of Bella and me.

Inside of the card reads, "To my Mummy, happy seventeenth birthday. I love you with all my heart and you are my everything. All my love and kisses, your Bella xxxxxx", I read out loud.

I can feel my eyes welling up as I give Bella a big kiss. I turn to glance at Aunty and see a tear escaping down her cheek.

"What a truly clever girl you are Bella writing those beautiful words to your Mummy", says Aunty as she gives Snowy a hug.

Bella has hold of the paper my present is wrapped in. Snowy is beside her sniffing it in a very inquisitive way. I laugh as Bella gently nibbles away and pulls a largish piece off which drops down to the floor. Snowy immediately picks it up and looks so funny with a piece of wrapping paper hanging out from his mouth.

"Here. I will take that. Thank you for picking it up Snowy. What a helpful and good boy you are", says Aunty warmly as she retrieves it quickly from him.

Bella is eager to find out what is inside the paper even though she should know as she bought it!

She pulls the remaining paper off to reveal a beautiful black and red rucksack. This is exactly what I needed. My old one has been sewn up so many times, and Mum has been threatening many a time, she is going to put it in the bin.

Intrigued, I open the main compartment to see a flat, white, square envelope. I pull it out. There is no message on the front.

I open it eagerly and grin.

"Fantastic", I exclaim! "I have L plates to put on Mums car so that I can learn to drive".

"How cool is this? Thank you so much Bella. I absolutely love my gifts and my card. Bella it goes without saying how much I love you too", I say as I wrap my arms tightly around her again.

"Right, shall we go and get that cuppa and you can open your other cards and presents?" asks Aunty.

I kiss Bella and Snowy before trotting back to the house alongside Aunty.

I have some truly beautiful cards from my family and friends.

I open Sophie's card and read it out loud.

"To my awesome best friend. I have booked Laura and her horse-box to take me, you, Flash and Bella for an afternoon ride along the beautiful beaches at Camber Sands. Let's get a date in the diary. Happy seventeenth birthday matey, love ya, Sophie and Flash xxx"

"How wonderful is that?" exclaims Aunty.

"Absolutely amazing, this is an awesome present and something to look forward to. I must text her in a minute to thank her", I grin back.

My next card to open is from Mum, Dad and Suki.

As I open it, two small white envelopes drop out.

"To our darling daughter, we cannot tell you how proud we are of everything you have achieved. Happy seventeenth birthday Emily, love always Mum, Dad and Suki xxxxx"

I open the first envelope, and I am thrilled beyond words. My Aunty, Uncle and Nan and Grandads have clubbed together with Mum and Dad and have bought me a course of twelve driving lessons with a local driving school.

The next card I open has twenty-five pounds inside with a message.

I read it out. "Happy Birthday dear. Here is the money you need for your theory test. I am counting down the days until you pass your driving test. Just think you will be able to drive my horsebox and chaperone me around in my old age. Love and warmest wishes Mrs Evans x".

Aunty is laughing out loud

"Mrs Evans has a great sense of humour", she smiles.

"I am sure if the two of you met, you would get on like a house on fire", I reply.

"Here you are, my girl. This is from me, the doggies, Tinker and all the ponies", she says as she hands me another envelope.

"This is confirmation to say your five sets of BSJA jumps will be delivered on Friday 29th August to your home address in Sussex", I read out, although I must say I am totally confused.

"But Aunty, I don't understand?" I query.

"A very good friend of mine is retiring from the circuit. She mentioned to me she needed a good home for her show jumps which have given her years and years of pleasure. I thought they would be ideal for you and Bella as I know you love to jump and haven't got any of your own. I have paid for a van to pick them up from Bristol and deliver them to your home", she explains.

"OMG", I screech with delight but suddenly go silent.

"But Aunty, you can't afford to buy jumps. I know how expensive they are as I am always keeping an eye out for cheap second-hand ones", I tell her.

"No, Ems. I didn't have to pay anything for the jumps. My friend just wanted them to go a good home. I promise, they haven't cost me a penny. I do appreciate you worrying about my finances though", laughs Aunty.

"Really? Oh Aunty, thank you so much. Bella and I will have so much fun with these and every time we use them, we will think of you", I smile back as I rush to get up and give her a massive thank you hug.

"You are more than welcome, my girl. Now off you trot as it is time for your session with Speckle. Freya isn't coming over until later this afternoon. She said she will be on time for our ride at three. You will have plenty of time to get washed and changed before our pub meal at one o'clock", she smiles.

Chapter 23

* * *

"Hᴉ sᴘᴇᴄᴋs. Hᴏᴡ ɪs ᴍʏ beautiful girlie today?" I ask her as she walks directly towards me.

I stand completely still whilst Specks sniffs my hair, then my cheek and tenderly licks my left hand.

"Do you know it is my birthday today? I am now old enough to learn how to drive a car. How amazing is that?" I say softly as my right-hand strokes gently up and down her neck, then lightly to her ears and slowly down between her eyes.

I swap my right hand for the body brush and I smile as it glides across her beautiful speckled coat.

The brush flows gently over her back and slowly down her rump.

"You are really enjoying this, aren't you my girl?" I ask her.

My left hand feels like a robot as it automatically provides her with nuts. The brush runs gently down her neck, onto her shoulder, past her forearm and down to her knee. In a leisurely manner I allow the brush to caress her cannon bone and down to her pastern. I am an inch away from her hoof.

"Good girlie", I tell her in soft and relaxed manner.

Specks is so relaxed as she happily munches the nuts, I offer her.

I stop for a slight second and allow the head collar which is over my left shoulder to roll slowly down my arm.

I have the head collar in my left hand, and I have no objections from Specks at all. I pull out a handful of nuts, the headcollar is underneath and whilst she is busy, as slowly as I possibly dare, I sneak my right hand under her neck and gently move the noseband part of the headcollar above her muzzle.

"Good girlie", I whisper to her as she concentrates on nibbling the nuts.

'*This is the best opportunity I am going to have*', I think to myself.

As slowly as I can, once again I stretch under her neck, gently taking hold of the strap to move it just enough so it sits lightly behind her ears.

"Good girlie Specks, you are being a true star today", I continue to tell her.

"I promise baby, you can have more nuts in a moment. Firstly, I need you to stand still and trust me", I inform her.

It only takes me a couple of seconds to put the strap through the buckle, and to double check it is safely fastened.

I cannot believe after all these years, Specks is at last wearing a head collar. This is the best birthday present I could have wished for. Red is most definitely the perfect colour for her, she really does look extremely bonny. Aunty certainly made a great choice when she bought this top of the range breakable head collar in anticipation that maybe one day, she would be able to get it on Specks.

"Specks, I cannot tell you how proud I am of you. This is the icing on the cake for me on my special day", I say to her as she gently takes the nuts, not seemingly phased at all.

"Come on baby, let's have a walk around", I tell her.

I take ten steps forward and wait. Specks is by my side. I turn and take ten steps to the right. Within seconds she is by my side.

"Oh Specks, you are one truly amazing girlie and are learning so quickly", I tell her as I gently wrap my arms around her neck.

The next moment is truly wonderful. Specks places her head tenderly over my left shoulder and let's out a beautiful sigh as though she is one very contented pony.

My eyes well up as I hold her close to me. Special moments like these are truly priceless.

'I wonder what Aunty going to say? I bet she won't believe me until she see's Specks wearing her stunning new head collar. Maybe I won't tell her. I will wait until she notices it for herself', I think to myself with a slight chuckle.

I seriously do not want this moment to end but we have no choice as Shadow trots over to us, closely followed by Fern.

"Hey you two. If you are thinking about getting up to more mischief, please don't", I tell them smiling.

Too late. Shadow has already picked up my body brush and is moving his head up and down holding it tightly in his mouth. Fern has moved closer to investigate and for a slight second from the angle I am looking, it honestly looks as if Shadow is grooming Fern.

I can't help but laugh at the pair of them.

Specks is still closely by my side. It looks to me as though she is tutting at their behaviour.

"I know, they are just like naughty children, aren't they?" I say to her.

"How about you swap my brush for a handful of nuts?" I ask Shadow.

He really does have a very naughty look in his eye. I am right. Before I have chance to grab some nuts from my bum bag, Shadow has taken off in full flight around the field with Fern chasing hot on his tail.

I look at Specks who is watching them in a very funny manner.

"Come here. Let me give you a kiss baby girl as I need to go and retrieve my brush. I will pop and see you this afternoon", I tell her as I tenderly kiss her velvety muzzle.

Do you know what? This is the first time I have kissed her muzzle. Today cannot get any better.

Chapter 24

* * *

"Ems. I hope your session went well earlier with Speckle. I have been busy thinking. How would you feel about maybe on your third week, letting me observe your daily sessions? I need to be able to connect with her like you do so I can continue your good work once you have gone home. I also think I would learn a lot from watching the two of you together?" asks Aunty.

"What a great idea Aunty. Of course, we would love you to join us. It would be my absolute pleasure. I will let you read my notes too as this will give you an insight into the daily progress we have been making", I smile.

"Marvellous Ems. Don't forget, I need you changed and ready to go in twenty minutes. I don't want us being late for your birthday lunch" Aunty tells me.

"We won't be late Aunty. I am just going to grab a quick shower. I will be with you in a jiffy", I reply back.

Twelve forty-five precisely and we are on our way.

My phone continues to beep with birthday text messages and numerous Facebook notifications.

It is going to take me ages to respond to everyone this evening. I must remember to skype Mum and Dad on time, and I need to type up my notes from today's session with Specks. I am really looking forward to logging this morning's progress.

Not long now until I will be having my birthday lunch followed by a fabulous ride on the beach.

Happy seventeenth birthday to me.

The lane is narrow in places and to my left a quaint little stream runs freely far away into the distance.

Ahead I can see a pub surrounded by wonderful green trees and an old wooden wishing well sitting proudly under the sign of the pub.

I smile.

'*What a fabulous location for my birthday lunch*', I think to myself.

Aunty skilfully parks the car.

"Come on birthday girl, out you get", she tells me.

"Going back hundreds of years, this used to be an old coach house and although it has been refurbished, the owners have managed to keep the warmth of a local and traditional country pub. Your Uncle and I enjoyed many a happy time here. In the winter we would sit around the open fire, enjoying the soft music playing in the background. Such good old days", she continues with a warm smile on her face.

I imagine the two of them chatting and drinking whilst watching the mesmerising flames dance around in the warmth of the fire.

'*Aunty must miss Uncle so much*', I think to myself.

I look up at the traditional thatched roof in amazement. You certainly don't see many buildings like this anymore.

I follow Aunty eagerly through the front door which has stained glass windows with so many vibrant colours. We are immediately greeted by a lady who looks to be in her early sixties.

"Good afternoon Pam. How wonderful to see you again", she smiles as she gives Aunty a welcome hug.

"Steph. I would like you to meet my niece, Ems. I still can't believe it myself, but she is seventeen years old today", smiles Aunty.

"How wonderful to meet you Ems and a very Happy Birthday to you", she says whilst giving me a hug too.

"I thought with it being such a lovely day, you might prefer to eat outside?" queries Steph.

Aunty and I look at each other and nod in agreement.

"Follow me, my lovelies", she says as she leads us through the huge bar area which is in the shape of an arc.

A stunning red carpet runs through the full length and width of this incredible building. To the left is the old inglenook fireplace sitting lifeless. This must be the one Aunty was telling me about. To the far-right, an identical one sits in the centre of a cosy snug area. The bar stools stand tall, made of dark wood with beautiful red upholstery seats to match the carpets. Numerous tankards hang on hooks all around the bar.

'I bet they take some cleaning', I think to myself, but accidently say it out loud.

"You are totally right about that Ems", laughs Steph.

"I try and polish at least two a week to keep on top of them. Some have been in my family for generations", she proudly tells me.

"How long have you been here?" I ask.

"I was actually born in one of the bedrooms upstairs Ems. This pub has been in our family for over three hundred years and has been passed down through the generations. I'd hoped this wouldn't change but my son is a solicitor living in Cambridge and my daughter is a vet in Worcester. To be honest the only interest they have in the pub is to drink all my profits when they visit", she grins.

Aunty and I both laugh loudly at the same time.

"Go on you first Ems", says Aunty as we walk towards the big open double doors which I assume must lead out into the beer garden.

I carefully watch where I am going as I follow Steph down the three concrete steps and turn to check Aunty is ok behind me.

I turn with a big grin on my face as I look around at the enormous garden which is laid out with numerous wooden picnic tables and surrounded by beautiful old looking trees.

My eyes are immediately drawn to a table in the far corner.

Chapter 25

✳ ✳ ✳

I TURN AWAY FEELING SLIGHTLY confused. I blink and look again.

"Happy Birthday Emily. Surprise, surprise', I hear a group of voices calling.

I am completely stuck to the spot I am standing on. I cannot move and my mouth is wide open.

"Woof, woof", I hear a familiar voice.

I cannot believe Suki is running directly towards me.

'What is Suki doing here?' I honestly cannot think straight.

I bend down as Suki appears in front of me and I open my arms to greet our excited baby. Her tail is wagging ten to the dozen as she continuously kisses my face. She is acting as if she hasn't seen me for years.

"You seriously didn't think we would miss your birthday, did you love?" I hear Mum's soft voice say.

I look up to see her eyes are welled up with tears as I wrap my arms tightly around her, hugging her as firmly as I possibly can. Tears of happiness also run uncontrollably down my cheeks.

"Now it is my turn to give my birthday girl a hug", pipes up Dad's deep voice.

"Happy birthday love", he whispers to me as he wraps his strong arms around me.

'I still cannot believe this is real. Surely this is just another of my bizarre dreams?' I think to myself but once again say it oud loud.

"I can assure you this is not a dream love. We drove up early this morning and are staying with you for the whole weekend", confirms Dad.

"Really?" I gasp.

Eventually, once Dad has let me go, I look around to see Aunty who is busy wiping her eyes and see Freya is standing next to her.

"Freya. What are you doing here?" I exclaim.

"You told me you weren't free until after three o'clock. How did you all manage to keep this a secret from me?" I enquire.

"Dad. You even told me you were dashing off to work when we spoke early this morning! You really fooled me", I continue laughing.

"Well me and Mum thought it would be lovely to come and see my big sister and you of course, on your special birthday", grins Dad.

"This is truly awesome", I reply.

"I can't wait for you to meet Aunty's gang. Oh Mum, you are going to fall head over heels with Tinker and her four dogs. Oh, and not forgetting our little donkey Snowy", I blabber in excitement.

Mum smiles warmly across at me.

"I can't wait to meet them all love", replies Mum.

Steph appears with our menus and has thoughtfully brought a fresh bowl of water for Suki.

After around fifteen minutes, due to Mum and Dad changing their minds numerous times, we are at last ready to order and as we wait for our food to arrive, we chat about how they all managed to plan this.

I can't resist going for the hand cut chips cooked in olive oil with a beautiful salad and some home-made bread.

I must say my meal is most definitely without doubt the best one I have ever eaten at a pub. Steph is absolutely thrilled to hear my words.

We all decline dessert, as we are feeling full to bursting.

"Guess what?" asks Aunty.

"My little brother said he is going to come on the beach ride with us later", she announces.

For a second, my mouth is wide open and I unable to speak.

"I know I haven't ridden since I was nineteen but surely it's just like riding a bike. You never forget?" laughs Dad.

"Wow Dad, this is going to be awesome. I have never, ever seen you ride", I exclaim excitedly.

"I hope I don't get a sore backside as I have to be back at work on Tuesday", he smiles.

"Don't worry about that bro, you can ride Crystal. Her saddle is synthetic, so it feels like you are sitting in an armchair", replies Aunty.

It is two-thirty before we arrive back at Auntys. We have decided to ride around five o'clock as this will give Mum, Dad and Suki a chance to settle in and unpack.

I watch in disbelief as Mum, Dad and Suki jump out of their car. I still cannot believe they are here.

"I will just go and get my gang. It is better for them to meet Suki outside before we all go inside", says Aunty as she trots off to open the front door.

Molly, Sugar, Lexy and Moss fly out like a bolt of lightning much to Suki's delight. A lot of bum sniffing is taking place and I smile as the five very happy dogs start to play bow and chase each other around like they have known each other for ages.

Dad is looking around with a warm smile on his face.

"I forgot how beautiful this place is", he smiles at Aunty.

I look over to Mum who is totally unaware that Tinker is right behind her.

"Oooohhh", she shouts out whilst jumping at the same time. Tinker just poked her backside with his horns and is merrily bleating at the same time.

I watch with a big smile on my face as Mum turns around to see Tinker for the very first time.

"Oh my. You must be the famous Tinker", she coos as she kneels known to say hello to him.

"Aren't you just adorable. Come here and let me give you a hug", she continues.

Mum has a big grin on her face and Tinker is looking back at her with his little tongue poking out. I knew they would fall in love.

Out of nowhere all five dogs come galloping flat out from around the corner. Suki is heading directly towards Mum with the other four in tow. Within seconds poor Mum is lying on the floor. She is being licked and jumped on but to my relief I can hear her laughing. I bet she is in her element at this present moment.

"Come on love, are you ok?" asks Dad as he offers his hand to help her up.

"Wow, now that is what I call a welcome", grins Mum as she brushes herself down.

Freya and I are giggling. We can't help it.

'Eeyore, Eeyore', calls Snowy.

"OMG, how cute does he sound? Is that Snowy calling?" asks Mum with a huge smile across her face.

"It certainly is Mum. Shall we get your cases inside first and then Freya and I can take you and Dad to meet all the ponies and Snowy. I bet Bella is going to be as shocked as I was to see you", I say.

Chapter 26

✳ ✳ ✳

'This way", I say as Freya, along with Mum and Dad follow closely behind me.

Suki has decided to stay inside with Aunty and her new friends.

As we walk towards the corral, Bella puts her head high in the air and is looking as if she can't believe who is walking towards her. She instantly canters towards us whinnying over, and over again. Snowy follows her closely attempting a little trot trying as hard as she possibly can to catch her up.

I am sure Bella is smiling as we make our way into the paddock. She walks directly over to Mum and I watch lovingly as Mum wraps her arms tightly around her neck. Who would have believed Mum had always been so scared of horses? That is until Bella came along.

"I have really missed you Bells", Mum tells her.

"It feels really empty without you at home and I miss popping out to see you for a cuddle", Mum tells Bella in a very soppy manner.

Bella has Mum in a head lock, but Mum is not complaining.

"Hey, what about me?" Dad asks Bella.

Bella releases a gentle whinny as she hears Dad's voice, and now it is Dad's turn.

Freya is busy giving Hope a cuddle and Mum is on her knees next to Snowy.

'Eeyore', he tells her.

"Oh my. You must be Snowy. I have to say you are the most beautiful donkey I have ever seen in my life. Just look at you", she tells him as she gently strokes his long and soft white ears.

"You are so dinky. I can see why everyone has fallen in love with you. You are definitely my type of guy", Mum continues in a silly and soppy voice as she plants a kiss on his muzzle.

"Has Snowy got a permanent home yet?" asks Mum, taking me completely by surprise.

"No. Not yet Mum. He is still recovering", I tell her.

"Well I think he should come and live with us, don't you love?" she blurts out looking at Dad.

Dad and I look at each other in astonishment.

"I must say he and Bella have become very good friends", I stutter, still not believing what Mum has just said.

"Hello, little guy. Wow, you really are a beauty aren't you", says Dad to Snowy as he kneels down beside him and Mum.

"Would you like to come and live with us?" Dad asks him.

'Eeyore', answers Snowy.

'I cannot believe I am seeing Dad acting all soppy like this. I am sure he only had half a pint of lager earlier'.

"Bells. What do you think? Would you like Snowy to be your little brother?" Mum asks Bella.

I seriously cannot believe what I am hearing. Freya has just arrived to hear the last part of the conversation and is looking at me in a questioning way. I shrug my shoulders and hold the palms of my hands up, trying to tell her, I haven't got a clue.

My parents seemed to have lost the plot, but I don't care, in fact I am over the moon.

"Ems. It would be ok with you, wouldn't it?" says Dad as he finally gets around to asking me.

A big grin emerges across my face.

"I would love Snowy to be part of our family Dad. We need to check with Aunty, but I am sure she will be thrilled to know he will have his own wonderful home with us all. It will also free up a place for another rescue pony in need. We would have to pay an adoption fee for him though", I blurt out excitedly.

"No problem, love. This little guy is worth every penny", smiles Dad as he and Mum continue to pamper Snowy.

"Well, I wasn't expecting that", I say to Freya as we both look at each other with a big grin across our faces.

"Time for a cuppa", says Mum as she kisses Snowy before she gets up, followed by a big kiss for Bella.

"Don't you want to meet the others first?" I ask Mum.

"Of course, I do, but I want to have a quick chat with your Aunty about Snowy", she grins as she grabs Dad's hand and literally drags him back to the house.

I glance at my watch to see it is quarter past four.

"Come on Freya, let's follow them. I can't wait to see Aunty's face", I say as we canter back to the house.

"Well, this is a delightful surprise", I can hear Aunty saying as we head towards the kitchen.

"Is that a yes?" screeches Mum.

"What do you think Ems?" Aunty asks, looking directly at me with a big smile across her face.

"Oh Aunty. It is a big fat yes from me", I grin back.

"You are on", shouts Aunty in sheer joy as she shakes Mum's hand confirming the deal. Next, she wraps both arms tightly around Mum to give her an enormous hug. I am slightly concerned as I am not sure how much breath she is squeezing out of her.

"What time shall we start getting ready for our ride?" I interrupt Aunty who thankfully releases Mum.

"Blimey. I hadn't realised the time", exclaims Aunty.

"Off you all go and have a fabulous time. I will look after everything here", assures Mum.

"I have some new potatoes and salad and a selection of other bits and bobs for our dinner. Feel free to have a rummage around", smiles Aunty.

"I can get it all prepared. Freya will you be joining us for dinner?" Mum asks.

"I would love to", replies Freya smiling.

"I am just going to get changed quickly. You get cracking and I will catch you up", says Dad.

Chapter 27

✳ ✳ ✳

I AM JUST ABOUT TO get Bella's tack, when I hear Aunty calling me.

"Ems. Ems, where are you?" she calls.

"Here Aunty, in the tack room", I reply.

"I cannot believe it. When were you going to tell me?" she asks in a very excited manner.

I haven't a clue what she is talking about.

"What do you mean Aunty? You are confusing me", I reply back to her.

"I have just said goodbye to Nick and Charlotte. They told me how they were totally gob smacked when they saw Speckle wearing a head collar and blimey Ems, so was I when they told me. Obviously, I didn't believe them, so I went to see for myself. OMG Ems. How on earth did you manage to do this? I am so, so, so, so, so proud of you", she babbles on, as she grabs hold of me and squeezes me tight.

I try hard to respond, but I am finding it difficult to get my breath. Thankfully it isn't too long before she releases me.

"I wanted it to be a surprise for you Aunty", I grin back.

"Doesn't she look gorgeous in red?" I continue.

"I still can't believe it Ems. Well done and yes red is most definitely her colour. Have you told Freya yet?" she asks.

"No. I want to see her face when she notices it for herself", I grin.

I cannot tell you how weird it is seeing Dad wearing a riding hat. I watch closely as Aunty holds Crystal whilst he mounts. He seriously looks like a professional as he gets into the saddle with ease and I am not just saying that cos he's my Dad.

"See bro. You've still got it", Aunty grins at him as he picks up the reins holding them casually.

Five-twenty and at last we are on our way.

Aunty and Dad lead the way with Freya and me following close behind.

'The sun is shining, the sky is blue, and Bella has just stopped as she's in need of a poo', I sing in my head but once again say it out loud.

"That is so funny Ems", laughs Freya who continues to have a fit of giggles.

"I love making little rhymes up", I laugh back.

"Make one up about me and Hope. Please Ems", she begs.

"Freya and Hope went for a hack, and can you believe Freya rode her bare back. Up the mountains and back down again, and thankfully on Hope's back, did Freya remain", I reply.

"OMG. How do you do that so quickly?" asks Freya in sheer amazement.

"I haven't got a clue. I get random words appear in my head and I rhyme them altogether. Simples", I laugh back.

Aunty and Dad haven't stopped laughing and chatting. They must have an awful lot to catch up on. I can taste sea salt floating through the air directly into my mouth. A soft warm breeze blows around my cheeks and through Bella's beautiful mane. We must be nearly there.

Freya and I have a few little trots. Dad is quite happy walking for now he'd told us earlier.

"Wow. Isn't this a truly magical sight", whispers Dad as we arrive at the edge of the beach.

Dad is feeling just like I did, the very first time Bella and I came here.

"Just look at the blue sea with the waves gently splashing around. Your Mum would love it here, and so would Suki", he continues.

Unfortunately, today there are lots of children and a few dogs playing on the beach. I am not too disappointed that we won't be able to canter along the golden sand as I have already had a truly awesome day. We will have plenty of time to ride here again over the next couple of weeks.

"Who fancies a paddle?" asks Aunty not waiting for an answer as she urges Amber on towards the water's edge.

Dad looks totally bewildered.

I seriously never imagined I would be riding into the Devon sea with my Dad.

"This is breath taking", grins Dad.

"Don't you remember coming to this beach late in your teens? You know the time you and your friends had a barbeque here, you got tipsy and called me to come and fetch you as you didn't want Dad to know you had been drinking alcohol?" smirks Aunty.

"That is why I probably don't remember then Sis", laughs Dad.

Bella has no hesitation at all in following Crystal, Amber and Hope into the calm blue sea for a paddle.

Crystal paws through the water powerfully with her front left leg.

Unfortunately, Bella and I who are directly behind them, take the full brunt of the flying sea water. Bella shakes her head in disapproval and Dad turns around to laugh at us both.

"Don't be a wuss Bella", smiles Dad.

"Isn't this just relaxing and therapeutic Ems? I honestly forgot how beautiful the coast is. Maybe I need to take more time out to enjoy and appreciate what is around us rather than constantly working all the time", he continues.

"Maybe we can ride together when we get home Dad? I am sure Mrs Evans would be happy to let you ride one of her horses", I tell him enthusiastically.

"Why not? Let's do it Ems. Your Mum can follow behind us leading Snowy when he is fully recovered. What do you think?" he grins.

A big smile emerges across my face.

"You are on", I reply.

"Ems, how wonderful is that going to be? You, your Dad and Mum spending quality time together? I wish my Mum would spend more time with me", Freya says looking a little sad.

"Why don't you talk to your Mum and tell her how you feel. Maybe the two of you could do something together even if it's just an hour once a week. I bet your Mum would like that too, the pair of you spending some quality time together", I reply.

"You are right. I will try and think of something we could do together so we can have some girlie time", says Freya who now has a smile back on her face.

I watch in sheer contentment as Bella muzzles the sea water, splashing her tongue around and snorting.

The four of us stand side by side looking around at the beauty which surrounds us. Our silence enables us to listen to the sound of the waves as they gently arrive at the edge of the shore. The sun's shimmering rays glisten onto the sea in the far distance. Seagulls screech overhead in their search to find and catch their next meal.

A memory pops randomly into my head. One of my favourite story books when I was younger was about a beautiful Mermaid. Her upper body was that of a human female and her bottom half had the most exquisite tail of a fish. As she swam, the scales on her tail would change colour and shimmer and glisten against the ocean. Her long stunning red hair and her mesmerising green eyes absolutely fascinated me. She had the voice of an angel and many human and animal friends.

Chapter 28

* * *

"WE'D BETTER START HEADING BACK", says Aunty.

"Ems. Are you ok?" asks Dad.

"Oh yes sorry. I was just thinking about mermaids", I smile back.

"Ems. You don't believe in mermaids, do you?" enquires Freya.

"Of course, she does Freya. Emily used to adore them when she was little. I would read her mermaid stories at bedtime. She would spend hours and hours drawing magical pictures to stick proudly onto her bedroom wall. If I remember right, she also had a matching mermaid duvet and pillow set", smiles Dad.

"Aw, that is so cute", laughs Freya.

"Stop teasing me", I tell her as we all turn to make our way back to the track.

The ride back home is at a very leisurely pace. Freya and I make plans for Sunday and Aunty and Dad constantly laugh and chat most of the way.

It is truly wonderful to see Dad so happy and relaxed instead of worrying about work.

It is just gone six forty-five, as we head through the black iron gates.

"Right my girls. Get yourselves untacked and sorted. We will see you back at the house", says Aunty.

As I walk Bella towards the corral, immediately something looks and feels wrong. The gate to the paddock is wide open. For a moment I panic and cannot think.

"Freya, the gates open. Snowy has escaped", I anxiously tell her.

"He can't have Ems. Come on let's double check to make sure he isn't in his stable", calls back Freya in a slightly frantic manner.

I urge Bella forward into the paddock and we ride around searching every corner whilst Freya checks the stables. Bella whinnies out loudly for her little friend.

"We need to go and tell Aunty. Hurry up Freya", I tell her urgently.

As quickly as we can, we trot over to the stables where Dad and Aunty are busy untacking Amber and Crystal.

"Aunty, Dad. Snowy is missing. We can't find him anywhere and the gate to the paddock is wide open. I promise I double checked it was locked before we left", I tell them in a quivering voice.

"Calm down for a second Ems. Let me and your Dad pop these two back into their stables. You and Freya take Bella and Hope back to their paddock and get them untacked as quickly as you can. Meet us back here in five minutes. Please don't worry, he can't have gone too far", reassures Aunty.

"I can't believe he has escaped", says Freya in a shaky voice.

"Come on let's get untacked as quickly as we can. The sooner we start searching, the better", I reply.

"You two go and look in the barn and check all around the sand school. Your Dad and I will start searching the big field. There is no way he can get out of the grounds as everywhere is completely escape proof", Aunty reassures us once again.

I let out a huge sigh of relief.

But where is he?

Freya and I look high and low. Snowy is nowhere to be seen.

Aunty and Dad come to find us at the sand school.

"This is really bizarre. There is simply no sign of him", says Aunty in a very confused manner.

"Why don't we pop and ask Mum when she last saw him?" I suggest.

"Come on. Let's go", says Aunty as me, Dad, Freya trot after her.

I can hear Bella in the distance constantly whinnying for her friend.

"Ssshhh", says Aunty as she comes to an abrupt halt.

"Did you hear that?" she whispers.

We stand still but cannot hear anything at all.

"I am positive I heard Snowy calling", she says as we continue to make our way to the house.

We literally throw open the front door and rush into the hallway.

We come to an abrupt halt and stand looking in disbelief.

I honestly cannot believe what I am seeing.

'Eeyore', says Snowy as he lifts his head up to look at us.

Can you believe Snowy is in Aunty's kitchen with Mum, Tinker and the five dogs?

Dad, Aunty, Freya and I look at each other with our eyes and mouths wide open.

"Great, you are all back. I hope you had a wonderful ride", says Mum in a very casual manner.

"We did thank you love. We have just spent the last twenty minutes anxiously looking for Snowy. We thought he'd escaped", replies Dad.

"You are silly. Look, he is fine love. He is such a little gem and has been helping me prepare the dinner", says Mum with a smile on her face.

I don't know whether to laugh or cry at this precise moment.

"After you left, poor Snowy started braying. After the third time I went to check on him and he stood pathetically looking at me with his big almond eyes. I found his head collar and bought him back to the house with me. He has been such a good boy", says Mum innocently.

Once again, the four of us look at each other. Aunty is the first one to cave in. Her laughter is beyond hysterical as Dad follows suit, then Freya, then me. The hallway is full of uncontrollable giggling.

"What are you all laughing at?" asks Mum innocently, which makes us laugh even louder.

Dad is the first one to compose himself and speak.

"Look love. Donkeys do not normally live inside houses", he smiles tenderly at Mum.

"Why not? He has been no trouble at all? In-fact Tinker, him and the others have got on famously", she replies.

Freya and I are bent over, still unable to control our giggling.

Aunty is busy wiping her tears of laughter away.

"Emily. Why don't you and Freya take Snowy back to his paddock?" asks Dad.

"I need to give him a kiss first", says Mum as she gently holds his little head, whilst planting a kiss tenderly on his muzzle.

"Come here my little bubba. I promise Mummy will pop and see you before bedtime my little baby.", she continues.

I cannot believe how smitten Mum is with Snowy.

Freya and I turn away, knowing that if we looked at each other, we would burst out laughing again.

"Come on Snowy. Let's get you back in your paddock with Bella and Hope", I tell him as I attach his lead rope and head off through the hallway.

Suki barks as I lead his new friend away. Snowy immediately stops, turns his gorgeous little head and Eeyore's back to him.

As soon as Freya, Snowy and I are out of the house, the infectious laughter starts all over again.

"I have never, ever, seen anything so bizarre", giggles Freya.

"Me neither. I am sure Mum has completely lost the plot", I reply.

Bella looks happy to have Snowy back in the field, and it isn't long before they settle down to graze alongside Hope.

We make our way back to the house to hear the kitchen is still full of laughter.

Chapter 29

✳ ✳ ✳

"There you are birthday girl", grins Joseph, as he makes his way towards me.

Within seconds he has literally swept me off my feet. I am beginning to feel slightly dizzy as he continues to spin me around and around in his muscular arms.

I am relieved when at last I am finally set back down on my feet.

"I bet you need a Joseph hug too, don't you Freya?" he says with his beautiful white teeth grinning directly at her.

Before Freya has time to answer, he immediately lifts her off the ground as if she is as light as a feather and spins her around and around and around. By the time her feet are firmly back on the ground, I have to say as usual after a Joseph hug, she looks truly hot and flustered.

"I have just spoken to your Dad Ems. Would you like to know what my birthday gift to you is?" he asks.

"I wasn't expecting a gift Joseph", I reply.

"I am going to give you, your very first driving lesson in a little car I have. I will take you to some private land I know which isn't too far away, and on lesson one I will teach you the basics. What do you think my beauty?" he continues.

"Really? Oh wow, yes please. That would be truly fabulous. Thank you very, very, very much", I grin back at him.

"Ok we will get a date in the diary for next week", he smiles.

Joseph is thrilled to be asked to stay for my birthday dinner and Freya can't help herself as she constantly flirts with him. More embarrassingly for me, Mum flirts with him too.

Oh well.

"Happy Birthday to you, Happy Birthday to you, Happy Birthday dear Emily, Happy Birthday to you", everyone sings loudly as Mum carefully carries over a beautiful white cake. Proudly sitting on the top is a photo of me and Bella.

How cool is this?

"Make a wish Ems", urges Mum as I watch the flames on the seventeen candles, flicker and dance in front of me.

I take a deep breath, blow out the candles in one go and close my eyes.

'I wish, I wish, I wish.........'

It is nearly nine-thirty by the time Freya and Joseph leave to go home and the washing up is all done. Joseph has kindly offered to give Freya a lift home. I hope she behaves herself.

Mum and Dad have popped out to give Bella and Snowy a goodnight kiss and are closely followed by five happy dogs and one very happy goat.

By ten o'clock, I am feeling absolutely shattered. I say a big thank you to everyone, give them each a hug and a kiss and wearily make my way off to bed.

I am sure I will sleep well tonight.

'What a fabulous birthday I have had', I think to myself as my eyes begin to close.

Chapter 30

✳ ✳ ✳

I OPEN MY EYES, TRYING hard to remember what day it is. I suddenly recall the events from yesterday. What an amazing birthday I had.

I jump out of bed and get washed and dressed as quickly as I can. It is only five past seven, but I can't wait to see Mum and Dad.

"Morning love", calls Mum as I appear in the kitchen to see her and Aunty laughing and chatting over a cup of coffee.

"Morning Ems. I hope you slept well", says Aunty.

"I certainly did", I reply as I give them both a kiss and a morning hug.

"Where is everyone?" I ask.

"Well your Dad is having a lie in with Suki, Molly, Lexy, Sugar and Moss. I popped my head around the door earlier, only to see Tinker lying on my side of the bed with his head on my pillow. Look at this photo I took. How cute is this?" asks Mum showing me the picture on her phone.

"That is a gorgeous photo Mum. I would love to see Dad's face when he opens his eyes to find there are six altogether in his bed. I will tell you from experience, it is very difficult to get them off once the doggies have taken residence. Isn't that right Aunty?" I chuckle.

"It certainly is Ems", laughs Aunty.

"What are your plans for today?" Aunty asks me.

"Well I didn't get around to typing my notes up from my session with Specks yesterday. Freya is coming over around mid-day and we were wondering if we could do a little more jumping practice before tomorrow. You will be coming won't you Aunty? What about you and Dad, Mum?" I ask.

"Of course, we will be there", they both say in unison.

"Nicky and Jess will be here around nine to help out, so I may take the opportunity to take your Mum and Dad for a long walk down by the river with the dogs", says Aunty.

"Fabulous. Mum you are going to love Nicky and Jess, they have so many funny stories to tell", I smile.

"How about I give your Aunty a break and cook you all a late breakfast for around eleven-thirty?" says Mum.

"Now that would be an awesome treat for me", grins Aunty.

"Shall I nip off and get my typing up to date and when Dad gets up, I can have another cuppa with you all before I go and work with Specks", I smile.

"Off you go then love", smiles Mum.

Half an hour later, I am back in the kitchen. Dad is at last up and is sitting at the table laughing away with Mum and Aunty.

Suki is the first one to see me and literally nearly bowls me over in excitement. What a beautiful girl she is.

"Morning Dad", I say to him as I reach over to give him a kiss.

"Did you sleep well?" I ask.

"Well Emily. I could not believe what I was seeing when I opened my eyes. The first thing I saw was Tinker's cute little head laying on your Mums pillow. He was just staring at me with his little tongue poking out. To be honest he gave me a real fright as I was expecting your Mum's face to be there, not that of a goat", he laughs.

I visualise this in my head and laugh out loud.

"After I got over the shock of your Mum turning into a goat overnight, I tried to move but I couldn't. I had all five dogs on top of me. I asked them politely to let me get up. No chance. No word of a lie Emily, they were literally having a licking competition on my face", he continues trying hard not to laugh.

"That is really funny Dad. Lesson learned. In future you will have to remember to close your bedroom door", I tell him.

Aunty seems to be engrossed on her phone.

"I am sorry. I don't mean to seem rude, but Val has just text me. She has received a call from a lady who is very concerned about two ponies she came across about an hour ago. It sounds like they have been dumped on some common land. Val is going to find out more and get back to me as soon as she can", says Aunty.

"That is disgraceful", says Mum tutting and shaking her head from left to right.

"Is it a possibility you may have to bring them here?" I ask Aunty.

"We will have to wait and see Ems. I will let you all know when I hear back from Val, but we will have to be on standby and be ready to go if our help is needed", she replies.

"Let me know when you hear anything Aunty. I will get cracking with my session with Specks just in case we need to dash off at short notice", I reply.

"I am going to nip off and fill up the lorry with diesel as I only have a quarter of a tank. I haven't a clue where the ponies are, so I'd better be prepared", she says.

I give them all a kiss and make my way over to give Bella, Snowy and Hope a morning hug.

"Good morning you three. I hope you slept well?" I ask as I wrap my arms around Bella's warm and silky neck.

'Eeyore', replies Snowy.

"Right my babies. I need to go and work with Specks, but I will pop back to see you all later. Bella, Aunty and I may have to go on another rescue mission. I will let you know when I hear any updates", I tell her.

I am positive she has just winked at me once again.

I reload my bum bag, grab my body brush and a manage to find a spare lead rope.

As soon as I open the gate to the field, all four cheeky foals come flying towards me.

"Good morning to you all. I hope you are going to try and behave yourselves today", I inform them as I roll a handful of nuts across the field to keep them occupied.

I turn to see Specks is at the far end of the field by one of the shelters. I watch as she lifts her head, lets out a gentle whinny and starts walking directly towards me.

"Good morning my girlie", I say to her as we meet in the centre of the field.

Another gentle whinny escapes, her little nostrils flicker in happiness.

"Oh Specks, you really are one special girl", I say to her as she gently licks my hand.

My right hand reaches up to the top of her neck and smoothly glides down to her shoulder, across her withers and over her back. She doesn't seem at all bothered.

I offer her some nuts as I slowly run my hand down her shoulder to her knee until I am touching her hoof.

"Good girlie", I tell her as she shuffles her leg slightly.

"I bet that tickles you doesn't it?" I smile.

I trade my left hand for the body brush and as slowly as I can, turn the direction of my body. My right hand offers her nuts whilst the body brush slowly sweeps down her neck on her off side. This is the first time I have attempted to groom this side.

Her mane certainly needs a good combing, but I will save that for another day. I need to get her used to me grooming each side of her comfortably first.

Her little body quivers as my brush slides over her back.

"It's ok Specks. I bet this feels strange to you, me grooming this side, doesn't it?" I ask her.

I take my time and continue to talk to her in a soft soothing voice.

"Specks. How would you feel about me attaching the lead rope onto your head collar so we can go for a little stroll?" I ask.

I slowly swap sides and continue to feed her from my left hand.

I keep my breathing steady as I untie the lead rope which I have around my waist.

For a slight moment Specks stops eating.

I continue to talk to her as I cautiously attach the clip onto the bottom of the head collar.

She jumps back.

"Good girlie", I tell her as I hold the lead rope, as loosely as I possibly can.

"Come on Specks. Let's have a walk around", I say.

I wait patiently until she is back at my side. I take two steps forward making sure I put no pressure on the lead rope. Specks follows. Within minutes we are walking around the field side by side with me holding the lead rope loosely.

I am absolutely thrilled and very proud of Specks.

I stop as my phone beeps.

"One second", I tell her as I look at my phone.

A message from Aunty, "Ems can you pop back to the house as soon as you can? x".

I wonder if this is about the two ponies who have been dumped?

"Specks I am going to have to cut our session short today. I am truly sorry, but Aunty needs my help.", I say to her whilst I gently unclip the lead rope.

She whinnies to me as if she is giving me her seal of approval.

I gently kiss her on her soft velvety muzzle before turning to make my way back to the house.

I am truly amazed to see Specks behind me and I cannot believe she is following me all the way to the gate.

How fabulous is that?

Chapter 31

* * *

I GALLOP TO THE HOUSE as fast as I can.

"Your Aunty is in the office love", says Mum as I rush through the kitchen at the speed of lightning.

"Ems there you are. Come on we need to go. Val called to say the two ponies look frail and weak, so we need to leave now", says Aunty urgently.

"I have asked Jess and Nicky to get the stable next to Snowy's bedded down. Your Dad is just grabbing two headcollars and some food. Come on, we must go", she continues.

"How far away are they?" I ask.

"About a forty-minute drive Ems. Could you grab the flask of coffee your Mum has made, and I will meet you at the horsebox", she replies.

"Yes Ma'am", I salute.

"Make sure you take care. I will delay breakfast until you get back", says Mum as she gives me a quick hug.

I glance at my watch to see it is nine fifty-five. Dad, Aunty and I are on our way.

"Has Val told you anything else about the two ponies?" I ask Aunty.

"Not much Ems, although she did say we would definitely need Adam to visit as soon as we get them home. I have messaged him, and he has replied to say he will be on stand-by", she says.

"I have never been involved with anything like this", says Dad.

"Your very first rescue mission Dad", I smile at him.

The journey goes quickly as we chat, and Aunty reels off story after story about how mischievous Dad was when he was younger, much to his embarrassment.

I cannot believe Dad drew graffiti all over his bedroom walls and even on the ceiling too. Aunty said he used to get hold of the curtains all around the house and swing on and off them pretending to be a monkey. His favourite party trick was continuously sliding down the bannister rail, holding his hands out wide, laughing his head off scaring the life out of my Aunt and his Mum.

"Look there's Val", points Aunty as we come to a halt.

I can see a crowd of people standing around on this derelict piece of land. I can just about make out two small ponies about twenty feet away.

I quickly pop into the back of the horsebox to grab the head collars and the two buckets containing some Chaffe and nuts.

The three of us head over as quickly as we can to where the small group of people are gathered.

"Excuse me", says Aunty as she makes her way through with Dad and I following closely.

What I see next is truly shocking. Two bay ponies with matted manes, gungy eyes and ribs showing through their neglected bodies stand before me. They can only be around twelve hands high.

"There you are Pam. Thanks for coming so quickly", smiles Val.

"Poor babies", says Aunty as she looks them over.

"We have asked around, but no-one has seen anything. These two were certainly not here yesterday the locals have told me", Val informs us.

"Well looking at the terrible state they are in, we need to get them home as soon as possible", states Aunty.

"Are they able to walk?" asks Dad in a very quiet voice.

I think he is in shock.

"They can walk but only just. It looks like one of them may have arthritis, poor love", says Val.

"Ok. I will go and get the horsebox and get as close as I can. Ems, can you get the head collars on them ready please?" she asks as she turns to fetch her lorry.

"Hey, you two, my name is Ems", I say in a very soft voice.

"I am going to gently put a head collar on you and then we are going to help you into the horsebox. We will take you home with us and get you tucked up into a warm and cosy stable", I continue.

I look over to see Dad is busy helping Aunty pull the ramp down. I am thrilled to see the horsebox has been made ready, with straw on the floor and two hay nets hung up full of sweet smelling, fresh hay.

"Could everyone move back please and keep quiet whilst we try and load the ponies into the box?" Val quietly asks the people who are present.

They immediately do as she asks and step back with looks of horror and disgust on their faces at the sight of the two ponies.

"We will try and lead them in together side by side as it will be less stressful for them", says Aunty.

Dad and Aunty stand about a foot away, each shaking a bucket.

The one I am holding takes a very unsure step forward.

"There we go, that's it", I say in a very calm voice.

Val is gently coaxing her pony who has now taken one step forward.

Aunty and Dad hold a handful of the mix out in the palm of their hands and offer it to the ponies.

To start with they look unsure but within seconds they have eaten it. I watch as Aunty and Dad smile at each other.

"Come on baby", says Dad as he holds out another handful of mix whilst taking a step backwards.

It works. Val's pony has taken another step towards Dad and gets to eat the mix. Aunty copies and my pony moves one step forward.

It takes about fifteen minutes to get them to where the ramp awaits.

"Hold on. Let me pop some straw down onto the ramp for them. It will make it look much more inviting", says Aunty.

"Come on, just one more step and you will be nearly there", I encourage my pony.

Val's pony takes one step forward, puts one leg on the ramp and immediately steps backwards.

"Hey, it's ok. There is no hurry, just take your time", says Val in a very soothing voice.

Aunty shakes the bucket.

"Come on. I know you want this", she smiles to my pony.

Result. One step forward, we are almost on the ramp. Aunty takes another step backwards and we take one step forward. At last we are safely on the ramp. Aunty gives my pony a handful of food from the bucket.

Aunty shakes the bucket again. This time we take two steps forward. Not far to go now.

Dad gently shakes his bucket. Val's pony is at last standing on the bottom of the ramp.

"Come on sweetheart. Nearly there", smiles Dad as he feeds the pony a handful of food.

Aunty shakes her bucket once more and my pony takes two very slow steps forward and we are inside the horsebox.

I have a big grin across my face.

"Come on sweetheart. You can do this", Dad is saying in a very soft voice as he gently shakes his bucket.

One step, two steps and at last Val's pony is safely inside too.

"Could you hold the lead rope so I can get the ramp up as quick as possible?" says Val handing it across to Dad.

Aunty slowly makes her way down the ramp to help Val. Dad and I let our ponies eat the remaining food in the bucket and continue to talk to them soothingly as the ramp goes up.

"All locked and safe", calls Aunty.

I am positive I can hear some cheering from outside. It must be the people who were concerned for the ponies.

Dad and I look at each other with a big smile on our faces.

"We did it", I say to him.

"We certainly did Emily. What an amazing experience that was. I can't wait to get them home and see what the vet thinks, poor loves", says Dad.

"Me too. I get so angry sometimes. What sort of person could do this? Leave two innocent ponies in the middle of nowhere to fend for themselves?" I say angrily.

"Absolutely sickening", he replies in a very sad voice.

Chapter 32

* * *

THE JOURNEY HOME SEEMS TO take forever. I keep a very close eye on the ponies. I must say the pair of them look very pitiful and sad. This is truly heart breaking.

Adam is going to meet us at home and Aunty has messaged Freya to move Bella and Hope into the big field for now. Aunty has told Mum much to her delight, with this being an emergency, she can take Snowy into the house. We need it to be as calm and quiet as possible, whilst Adam checks them over and he is sure they haven't got anything that could be contagious to our other ponies.

It is twelve thirty as we pull in to the yard and I can see Jess, Nicky and Freya anxiously waiting for us.

"Adam is ten minutes away. This will hopefully give us enough time to get them settled into their stable", says Aunty as the horsebox comes to a standstill close to the corral.

I jump out as fast as I can.

"Hey kiddo", smiles Jess as she gives me a welcome back hug. Nicky follows suit and so does Freya.

I am totally hugged out!

I quickly introduce Jess and Nicky to Dad before he rushes around to the back of the box to help Aunty put the ramp down.

"Freya, Ems", calls Aunty in a soft voice.

"Could you two get hold of a pony each. Dad and I will try and coax them slowly down. Jess, Nicky, would you be able to put some more nuts and Chaffe into these two buckets please?" asks Aunty.

Freya and I slowly walk up the ramp.

"Look at you two. Aren't you just beautiful? We are going to get you settled in and make sure you have some wonderful food and everything else you need", whispers Freya.

I gently take hold of one lead rope and Freya has the other.

I hadn't realised how much alike the two of the ponies look.

I wonder if they could be related?

Dad and Aunty gently shake the buckets. We take two steps forward and allow them to have a mouthful of food.

Slowly, slowly we make our way down the ramp side by side, and at last make it onto the yard area.

The two ponies look around probably wondering where they are. My pony lets out a very pathetic whinny.

"Come on, this way", coaxes Aunty as she walks backwards with the bucket.

Six steps, five, four, three, two, one and we are safely in the beautifully bedded down stable. I notice hay on the floor in the two far corners of this thick golden bed that is awaiting our new arrivals.

"There you go. I bet you like the look of this stable, don't you? The two of you are safe now. Welcome to your new home", I whisper to my pony as I gently stroke his or her neck.

"You stay there my girls. I think Adam has just pulled up", informs Aunty.

Freya's pony has led her towards the hay and is happily munching away.

Here comes Adam with his medical bag and Aunty and Dad following closely behind.

"Good afternoon Ems & Freya. Now who have we got here?" he says.

"Ems, Let's have a look at your pony first", he continues as he slowly walks towards us.

I continue to talk gently to my pony whilst stroking him/her softly down the neck.

He listens to my pony's heart, checks the teeth and examines this poor little soul thoroughly.

"Ok. This little beauty is probably around twenty-two years old. She has slight swelling in her two front legs, which could mean the early stages of arthritis. Her heart is strong, but she is very underweight and slightly dehydrated. I will clean up her eyes and prescribe flea & worm treatment and I will give her a shot of anti-inflammatories to help ease some of the tenderness she may be feeling. I am confident she has been a riding pony and was probably dumped due to her showing early signs of lameness. She will need to follow a strict and nutritious diet. I will also add some joint supplements to help too. Hosing her legs down with cold water twice daily will help reduce the swelling and massaging her legs will also be of benefit. She doesn't have a microchip", he informs us.

No microchip doesn't surprise me. I sigh with relief and I am so thankful we are going to be able to get her back to looking like the happy pony she should be.

"Your turn now", says Adam as he slowly walks across to Freya and her pony.

After ten minutes of thorough examination, Adam stands up to have a stretch.

I cannot believe how well behaved these two have been.

"This little fella is around seventeen years old. It wouldn't surprise me if they were in fact mother and son. He also has a strong heartbeat and apart from being seriously underweight, he isn't doing too badly, considering. He doesn't have a microchip either. I will run some blood tests, but I doubt we will find anything too much to worry about. They both need their teeth rasped which I will do in a couple of weeks once they have settled in. A visit from the farrier could be beneficial too. What I would suggest, is to let them rest where they are just for today. This will give them chance to settle in and time for me to run their blood tests back at the lab. From tomorrow you can start hosing down the mare's legs. If I were you, I would get them out into the field along with the others on a permanent basis as soon as possible. Ponies who show signs of early stages of arthritis need to keep moving around. Not only will this help to reduce the swelling, it should also improve the circulation to her legs", he continues.

I look across at Aunty who is smiling with relief and Dad has a big grin on his face too.

"You will need to let me know when you have thought of names for them so I can get their certificates ready", says Adam.

"Mix and Match", blurts out Dad.

"What great names bro", says Aunty.

"Well they look so much alike, the names just jumped into my head", says Dad excitedly.

"Mix and Match it is then. Ems yours is Mix and Freya your boy is Match", laughs Aunty much to Dad's delight.

"That's all sorted then", grins Adam.

"Right. Pam if you could get my other bag from my car, I will take the blood samples now, clean up their eyes, give them their worming and flea treatment and a shot of anti-inflammatories for Mix", he continues.

I cannot believe how good Mix and Match have been. Maybe they are relieved to be in a safe place at last, with access to food and water. Aunty is one hundred percent sure they are Welsh Section A ponies. Apparently, the maximum height is 12.2hh. Mix is 12.1hh, and Match is 12.0hh. It is very sad to think these two have probably worked hard as riding ponies for most of their lives, giving pleasure to many children over the years and then just dumped at the first sign of illness. I cannot tell you how angry this makes me feel.

After Adam has given them the treatment they need, he heads off back to his clinic.

"What good ponies Mix and Match have been. Freya, Ems, if you can take their head collars off for now, that would be great. I think it is better to let them have some peace and quiet for a while", says Aunty.

"See you later my little Mix", I tell her before gently planting a kiss on her head.

Freya and I look at each other and smile as we lean over the stable door and watch them happily eating their hay before making our way back to the house.

"You really are a dark horse, aren't you? I cannot believe you kept that a secret from me Ems", says Freya.

"What are you talking about?" I ask her in a confused matter. I seriously haven't got a clue what she is going on about.

"Getting a head collar onto Speckle", she replies in a very excited manner.

"Ah, now I get it. I wanted it to be a surprise for you. I didn't tell Aunty either", I smile.

"Ems you are truly awesome. Never in a thousand years would I have expected to see that", she smiles.

"It was a joint effort between me and Specks. She is the superstar, Freya", I reply.

Chapter 33

* * *

THE SMELL OF SIZZLING SAUSAGES immediately fills the air as we walk into the kitchen.

Jess, Nicky, Dad and Aunty are sitting chatting around the table. Mum has a tea towel draped over her shoulder and is busy multi-tasking between the frying pan and the toaster.

"There you are love", says Mum as she glances over to me.

"Hi Mum. Where is Snowy?" I ask.

"Don't you worry love. He is out playing in the back garden with Tinker", she smiles.

"You two go and sit at the table. I will make you some coffee. Would you both like beans on toast?" asks Mum.

"Yes please", Freya and I say at the same time.

"Do you want a hand Mum?" I ask.

"No thanks love. I am enjoying myself and don't worry I have everything under control. Go and sit down and relax", she smiles back.

I pull up a chair next to Dad.

"Jess, I hear you are a police officer", says Dad.

"You are correct. Is there anything you want to tell me or need to confess?" she asks in a very serious tone.

"I have nothing to confess at all. I am a law-abiding citizen", he replies with a grin on his face.

"That's a relief then", laughs Jess.

"Jess" says Dad seriously. "Last week two policemen were called to the scene of a crime at a convenience store close to Brighton. One of them asked the manager to explain what had exactly happened. The manager replied, 'There is a man over there who is covered in cornflakes, I think he might be dead'. The first policeman frowned and said, 'That's very odd. Last week we found a dead guy covered in bran flakes and the week before another dead body covered in Weetabix'. The second police offer replied, 'Yes you are right. This is obviously the work of a cereal killer!'"

I cannot tell you how much laughing follows Dad's little joke. Jess and Nicky have tears of laughter rolling down their faces. Mum nearly drops Dads breakfast on the floor, Aunty is in uncontrollable hysterics and I nearly fall off my chair.

Eventually everyone settles down and it is agreed no more jokes at the table.

"For the time being", Dad whispers, and winks.

'Eeyore', calls Snowy as he makes his way across to the table.

"Hey, my baby boy", coos Mum.

We watch with our mouths wide open as Snowy lifts his tail and the next moment we hear, plop, plop, plop.

"Oh dear", gasps Mum.

"Never mind, when you need to go, you have to go. Don't worry Mummy will clean it up for you", she continues.

Aunty's face is a treat. Her mouth is wide open in disbelief and this sets us all off laughing again.

"Freya and Ems. I think it might be time for Snowy to go back to the field, don't you?" she says when she can eventually speak.

"It's only a poo", smiles Mum which sets us all off again.

My ribs are aching from the laughter.

"Freya and I are going to do some practice for tomorrow so we will take Snowy back to his paddock on the way", I reply.

"What are you doing tomorrow?" asks Nicky.

I tell her all about the horse show.

"Nicky, why don't you ride Amber over to the show with the girls. You could even try a clear round with her", blurts out Aunty.

"I couldn't. It is such a long time since I have done any jumping", replies Nicky.

"You could practice with the girls this afternoon? Come on what do you think?" urges Aunty.

"Oh, go on Nicky, you must. It will be great fun for you", urges Jess.

"But I haven't anything to wear", says Nicky with slight panic in her voice.

"I know you have jodhpurs, I will dig you out a shirt and jacket as we are not far off the same size. All sorted then", grins Aunty.

"This is going to be great fun", I say happily.

"Come on let's take Snowy back and get tacked up", says Freya.

"Bye-bye my little baby. Mummy will come and see you later", she tells Snowy as she plants a soppy kiss on his head.

I glance at my watch to see it is four-fifteen as we make our way over to the school.

Dad and Jess are coming out to watch us whilst Aunty and Mum are going to spend some time with Mix and Match.

"I think we ought to do some warm up exercises first, don't you?" asks Freya.

"Sounds like a great plan", replies Nicky.

"I was reading through some of my science notes the night before last and found it very interesting. Horses and ponies need to warm up to get their muscles working. It is just the same as humans do. Say for instance you had been sat down all day and decided to go for a ten-mile run, your body wouldn't be prepared for it and your muscles would seize up. It's the same for horses and ponies. It makes sense doesn't it?" I say to them as we walk side by side.

Bella is walking beautifully around the outside of the sand school and even though she is eyeing the jumps, she feels very relaxed.

Bella and I start with twenty minutes of walk and trot transitions, until we are nice and warmed up before finally cantering on twenty metre circles on both reins.

Nicky looks awesome riding Amber and the two of them look to be having a fabulous time.

"Who wants to go first?" asks Freya.

"Nicky. You go first", calls Jess from the outside of the school.

Nicky looks at Freya and me, and we give her the thumbs up.

Nicky and Amber perfect the first grid with grace, and upon landing, Nicky pushes Amber into canter, and lines up for the double. They take off effortlessly and clear the jump perfectly with at least a foot to spare!

"Wow. Well done Nicky", calls Jess.

I can see Nicky has a massive grin across her face as she heads towards the second double. Once again, they clear it easily and turn towards the treble. Nicky collects Amber up, they have a clear round.

Dad and Jess clap loudly as Jess eases Amber down to a trot, then walk before finally halting with a bow.

"That was truly exhilarating", beams Nicky.

"I want to do it all over again. What a buzz that just gave me", she continues to say, whilst giving Amber a well done pat down her neck.

"Go on Ems. Your turn next", calls Freya.

I give her the thumbs up and off we go. We canter large as Bella is taking a very strong hold. We canter in a twenty-metre circle before I ease her back down to a trot, and she settles immediately. We trot large, before I line her up for the grid.

"Come on baby. We can do this", I tell her as she takes the first impeccably.

"Good girl", I tell her.

I line Bella up for the double. At this moment I feel perfectly in tune with her as I lean forward as Bella lifts the whole of her body weight with great ease, followed by a fabulous landing.

"Good girlie. We can do this Bella", I say with encouragement.

I have completely shut the outside world out. I am totally focussed on Bella and she seems to be listening to what my body is telling her. We have a bond that can never be broken.

I concentrate as we head towards the treble, and we literally sail over without fault. I am thrilled to bits and so proud of my Bella.

I can hear Dad and Jess shouting well done whilst clapping at the same time.

I am greeted by Nicky and Freya who are both grinning at me.

"Ems. That was an absolute pleasure to see. True perfection in fact. You made that look so easy. Well done to the pair of you", beams Freya.

"Nice one, Kiddo", smiles Nicky as she gives me a high five.

Once again, Freya and Hope put up a fabulous performance and we give them a round of applause.

"That was brilliant Freya. I am starting to get a tad excited about tomorrow", I smile at her.

Chapter 34

* * *

"IT LOOKS LIKE YOU THREE girls are having a whale of a time", says Aunty as she walks towards us waving something shiny in her hand.

"We all managed a clear round", I tell her with a big grin on my face.

"Well done. Now it is time for you to do some practice for the egg and spoon race", laughs Aunty as she waves around three shiny spoons whilst managing to produce three eggs magically from her bum bag.

"Jess, bro, could you come and give me a hand moving the jumps to one side?" she calls out.

"Egg and spoon?" questions Nicky in a slightly worried voice.

"Don't look so worried, it is just a bit of fun", Aunty assures her.

"Come on. Let's get the three of you in a line about six feet apart. I will then give you, your egg and spoon. You need to walk, and I mean walk to the other end, turn around and head back to me. If any of you go into a trot, you will have to come back to the start and begin all over again", instructs Aunty.

Freya and I smile at each other as Aunty hands us an egg and spoon each.

"Now be careful not to drop the eggs as I need them to make my Yorkshire pudding with tomorrow", she smiles.

"No pressure then", laughs Freya.

"On your marks, get set, go", calls Aunty.

I have the egg and spoon in my right hand and look to my left, then to my right and I am thrilled to see I am slightly ahead.

"Oh Ems. Wasn't your Dad's joke funny earlier? What is even more hilarious is when Snowy plopped all over the kitchen floor", I can hear Freya saying.

I think about it once again and laugh out loudly as I turn to grin at Freya.

Wrong move, I have lost my concentration and my egg is now laying in the sand.

"Woops", exclaims Freya with a big grin on her face.

"You did that on purpose, didn't you?" I call out to her.

"You snooze, you lose", she replies, momentarily turning back to look at me.

"Hahahaha, now that just serves you right", I tell her as I watch her egg fly off the spoon.

Nicky is already on her way back to the finish looking very calm and collected.

"And the winner of our egg and spoon race is, wait for it, Nicky and Amber", announces Aunty.

Aunty is trying to stifle her giggles at Freya's race tactics that backfired. I suppose it is quite funny.

"Now this is what I call entertainment", laughs Dad loudly.

Aunty retrieves our eggs which are not broken as she confesses, they are in fact hard boiled.

"Now you have warmed up. Let's try the sack race", announces Aunty with a big smile.

"Seriously?" I ask.

"Oh, come on Ems, it will be a laugh", says Nicky who is so happy to be at the top of the leader table in the gymkhana games.

Aunty nips off and quickly returns with three empty sacks.

"When I shout go, you must ride over as quickly as you can to retrieve your sack from the floor. You need to get into it as fast as you can and jump all the way back to the finish, simples", laughs Aunty.

We all look at each other and grin.

"I've got this", I tell Freya in a very serious voice.

"Whatever", she replies with a grin on her face.

"Right, on your marks, get set, go", calls Aunty.

I urge Bella on and from a standstill, she responds immediately as we canter effortlessly to the far end. I jump off as quickly as I can and pull the reins over her head. I am in my sack and jumping for dear life. I am totally focussed and well and truly ahead until I hear Freya's voice calling out.

"Pam. Aren't these the sacks we found in the corner of the barn?" she says slightly out of breath.

What? The spider barn?

I have a moment of sheer panic and accidentally drop Bella's reins. I am convinced I have something crawling on my face. I flap my arms and legs about as I try to scramble out of the sack at lightning speed. My foot gets caught and I cannot save myself from landing heavily on my backside. I jump up quickly and wipe my hands all over my face in a vain attempt to brush away anything that may be crawling on it.

I lift my head to see Freya jumping up and down in delight at the finish.

'Hold on a minute', I think to myself.

I can hear so much laughter around me. In fact, Freya is literally crying she is laughing so hard.

"I am not sure I would call that team tactics Freya, but I have to give it to you, you played that well", laughs Aunty.

"But you said the sacks were from the spider barn?" I question in disbelief.

"No Ems. They are not from the barn at all. I keep them inside the house, and I can assure you there are certainly no spiders in them", she continues.

I turn to see Bella looking at me. I point my finger directly at Freya and call out, "Freya, I am going to get you back for this".

"Bring it on", Freya shouts back as I fall flat onto the floor laughing.

I have to say that Freya, was certainly one step ahead of me this time.

"Now that is what I call a fun hour of entertainment", laughs Dad as he puts his hand on my shoulder.

"Freya are you staying for dinner?" asks Aunty.

"I am not sure I'd be welcome", she replies looking at me, pretending to look sad.

"Of course, you are silly. I must say your brain works very fast to come up with a way to divert my attention as quickly as you did. In fact, it was brilliant. Well done you", I tell her laughing.

"No hard feelings?" she asks.

"Don't be silly. Get a grip, we are good friends and always will be", I assure her as I hold my hand up for a high-five.

"Why don't you get your ponies washed down. Your Dad has gone to give Jess a hand clearing the fields. Oh, by the way, some good news from Adam. Mix and Match's blood tests have come back clear, so nothing to worry about", smiles Aunty.

"Wow, that is brilliant news", I respond with a big smile on my face.

"You can turn Bella and Hope back out into the paddock with Snowy and tomorrow I will move Mix and Match into the big field", smiles Aunty.

"Ok cool. We will see you back at the house shortly", replies Freya.

'Eeyore', calls Snowy as Bella whinnies back to him.

"Now you three be good and please try not to be too noisy as we have our two new arrivals resting over there in the stable", I tell them.

I am sure Bella understands what I am saying to her as she lifts her head over my shoulder for a hug.

We walk our ponies towards the hose and wash them down. They whinny in sheer delight, noticing they each have a lovely hay net full of sweet, smelling hay, tied to the fence with bailer twine, ready and waiting for them.

Freya and I walk over to the stable block, lean our heads over the door to find Mix is laid flat out, and Match has his head leaning over her shoulder. This is just one of the cutest things ever.

"I wonder if they are Mother and Son?" I say to Freya.

"Well, I suppose there is one way to find out. They could have a DNA test", replies Freya.

"Now that is a great idea. Why didn't I think of that? I will ask Aunty to find out how much one would cost and maybe we could try and somehow raise the money?" I reply excitedly.

We grin at each other with another high five.

Chapter 35

∗ ∗ ∗

DINNER IS FULL OF LAUGHTER.

'*This is what it is all about*', I think to myself with a big smile on my face.

Family and friends sitting around the table having a wonderful time together.

Jess and Nicky get up to leave.

"Thank you so much for such a wonderful dinner Ems Mum, but unfortunately we have to make a move now. We will see you all again tomorrow though", smiles Nicky.

"You are more than welcome and thank you for helping with the washing up", smiles Mum as she gives them both a hug.

"Here you go Nicky. I have put two blouses and three different jackets in this bag for you to try on", smiles Aunty.

"What time should I get here in the morning?" asks Nicky.

"The jumping classes start at eleven, so I think we should leave around ten as it will only take us around half an hour to hack over. I will tell Jamie to meet us outside his house at ten past ten as it is on our way", grins Freya.

"I know you wanted me to come along my girls, and I wanted to come and shout you on too, but I honestly don't think I will have time. I need to hose down Mix's legs and get her and Match settled in the field. Shadow and Fern's potential new owners have messaged to say they will be here around twelve tomorrow instead of three, so it is very important I am here", says Aunty.

"That is a shame, but we totally understand. Mum, Dad are you still coming?" I ask them.

"Bro, why don't you ride Crystal over to the show with the girls. It would be great fun for her, she would really enjoy it and you won't be the only guy as Jamie is going too", smiles Aunty.

"Go on Dad, it is going to be great and it means I can spend more time with you before you go home on Monday", I plead.

"Ok love, you have twisted my arm", smiles dad warmly.

"What time do you think your classes will start?" enquires Jess.

"Looking at the schedule, I doubt any of ours will be starting before twelve thirty", pipes up Freya.

"Well, why don't I get everything done here with Pam. I can then drive over with Mum in time to watch your classes. Pam, this will give you some quality time to spend with Fern and Shadow. What do you all think?" asks Jess.

"Now that sounds a perfect plan Jess", grins Aunty.

"Let's meet here at eight o'clock. This will give us plenty of time to get our ponies looking absolutely-fabulous", I grin.

I get a hug from Freya as Jess and Nicky are kindly giving her a lift home. I keep forgetting to ask her if she behaved herself when Joseph dropped her home. I must remember to ask her tomorrow.

"Aunty, how much would a DNA test cost?" I ask her.

"Why do you ask?" Ems.

"Freya and I were thinking earlier. Wouldn't it be wonderful to find out for sure if Mix and Match are one hundred per cent Mother and Son?" I reply

"Well there's a thought. I suppose I could ask Adam. You are right, it would be nice to know", she replies.

"Freya and I are happy to find a way to raise the money", I smile.

"Let me message Adam and as soon as I find out, I will let you know", she grins back.

"Fingers crossed for Fern and Shadow tomorrow Ems. Dee, her husband and their two children are all coming to visit. I do sometimes change the rules slightly for foals. If I see the love and connection between them all tomorrow, I will let the pair of them go during next week. As the two of them will be together, I feel the sooner they get settled into their new surroundings, the better it is for them", she continues.

"That makes sense Aunty. I can't believe how well they have all have come on in the past four months. You and Freya have done amazing work with them. Fingers crossed Trixy and Misty find a wonderful home too", I reply.

"Do you know where Mum, Dad, the dogs and Tinker are hiding?" I ask.

"I am sure your Dad mentioned they were going to take them all for a walk, and, afterwards pop over to spend some time with Snowy and Bella", she tells me.

"I might go and type up my notes from my session with Specks. I am going to do an early one with her tomorrow around seven as I would hate to miss even one day of my assignment", I say.

"That it what I love about you Ems. You are truly dedicated and give everything one hundred per cent. I am looking forward to shadowing the pair of you the week after next", Aunty responds.

"Now I am going to go and check on Mix and Match, give them some dinner and make sure they are settled in for the night. I haven't a clue where today has gone? I think we all need an early night tonight. Don't you?" she asks.

"You can say that again. The time just flies when I am here. There is always something to do and unexpected happenings taking place. Every day is a brand-new day to look forward to. It has been so lovely having Mum and Dad here too. I am learning new things about Dad I didn't even know", I exclaim.

"It really is good to see my brother so relaxed, laughing and joking. By the way, your Mum said she has spoken with Laura and she is very excited about meeting Snowy. Bless her, she also has a great heart as she isn't going to charge anything for taking Snowy back home with you and Bella. Your Mum really is smitten. Can you believe I have promised her that I will skype her every day once she has gone home, so she can see him?" laughs Aunty.

"No way. Really? Are you going to humour her?" I ask in disbelief.

"I have made a promise Ems, so yes I will", she grins.

It only takes me half an hour to type up my notes. There is still no sign of Mum and Dad, so I decide to head out and find out where they are.

It doesn't surprise me to find Mum sitting on the grass in the paddock with Snowy one side of her and Tinker the other.

'Eeyore', calls Snowy as he sees me approach.

"Hi, little fella. Are you getting lots of cuddles from your new Mummy?" I ask him.

"Oh, Emily love, isn't he just the best? I am going to miss him so much when we go home. I suppose I could always send your Dad home on his own and I could stay here with you, Pam and Suki. Now what a great idea that is", smiles Mum.

"What about work, Mum? Don't you have a big fundraising event next weekend for the shelter?" I ask.

"Oh drat. You are right love. Well, I am most definitely go shopping to get in everything he needs for when he comes home. I have even started writing a list", she tells me.

"Aw, that is sweet Mum. Where is Dad?" I ask.

"He has just taken the dogs for a good run in one of the spare fields. He should be back shortly", she replies.

I turn to see Bella walking towards us, letting out a little whinny as she saunters over. I can feel Tinker prodding my backside, much to Mums delight.

"Hey baby, how is my number one girl?" I ask her as I wrap my arms tightly around her neck.

"Guess what Bella? We are going to a show tomorrow and me and you are going to do some serious show jumping. Can you believe the first prize in each class is fifty pounds, second place thirty pounds and third place twenty pounds? Freya and Hope are coming too, so are Jasmine and Jamie, Nicky and Amber and your Grandad is joining us too riding Crystal. How cool is that?" I tell her.

Bella responds by leaning her head heavily over my left shoulder.

"Nanna and Jess are coming to shout you on too Bells", pipes up Mum.

Bella lets out a huge sigh.

'No pressure on me then for tomorrow' I am sure she is thinking.

"Right my baby. You rest and sleep well. It is getting late and we have a big day tomorrow. Try as hard as you can to keep clean", I tell her as I give her a goodnight kiss.

After a long hot bath, I cannot tell you how happy I am to be in bed at last. I listen to the silence around me, switch off my bedside light, my pillow is soft and cosy as I lay my head down.

Chapter 36

* * *

ARGH! MY ALARM IS BEEPING like crazy and even though I am half awake, it still makes me jump.

Six-thirty am and time for me to get cracking. I jump out of bed with a spring in my step as I think about everything we have got planned for today.

I wonder how Bella and I will get on in the show jumping?

Mum as usual is already up but everyone else is still tucked up in bed.

"Morning love. I heard your alarm go off, so I thought I would make you a cuppa before you start your day", smiles Mum as I give her a hug.

"Aw, thanks Mum. You are the best", I tell her.

"Is there anything you need me to do? I am going to put a little picnic together for later and prepare a lovely Sunday roast for this evening. Ems, your Dad has really surprised me this past couple of days, this little break has done him the world of good", beams Mum.

"I know Mum. I am really impressed with his riding and how confident he is in the saddle. I hope he will keep it up when we get home", I reply as I take a slurp of my coffee.

"Don't worry, between us we will make sure he does. The next two weeks are going to go very, very slow whilst I wait for you, Bella and Snowy to come home. I have been thinking although I haven't mentioned anything to your Dad yet. How would you feel if we took on a rescue goat like Tinker? He is just so cute", says Mum.

"The way you are going Mum, we will end up with a rescue sanctuary of our own", I laugh.

"Now, what a great idea that is", beams Mum.

"Mum, I was kidding. If you could pop out around nine-thirty to keep an eye on Bella whilst I get changed, that would be a great help. Thankfully Freya is lending me a show jacket. I certainly didn't think I would need one on this visit so mine is hanging in my wardrobe at home", I tell her.

"Freya is a lovely girl Ems. It is great to know you have someone of your own age to hang out with whilst you are here", she replies.

"Yes, it is Mum. We do get on really well and have an awful lot in common", I smile.

"Right I had better move my backside and get cracking", I continue as I wash my cup up.

"See you later Mum", I call as I head off out the front door.

"Morning Bella, morning Snowy", I call as I trot over to the paddock.

'Eeyore', answers Snowy.

"Oh Bella, look at the state of you. I cannot believe you have been rolling in dung, today of all days", I say to her. I look in dismay at the brown and green stains that cover her neck, mane and hind quarters.

"You are going to need a bath young lady", I tut at her.

Bella curls her top lip up at me as if she is laughing.

"Come here you. How could I ever be angry or get annoyed with my baby", I tell her as I wrap my arms tightly round her neck. She leans her head into my back as though she is giving me a hug back.

"Ok, a bath for you is now on the cards stinky", I continue.

"I will be back in an hour or so to get you looking presentable", I tell her as I kiss her muzzle, give Snowy a kiss and trot off to get my bum bag, body brush and lead rope.

The early morning sun feels warm already. I hope it isn't going to get too hot for the show today.

With my bum bag loaded, I trot merrily pretending to be a dressage horse all the way to the field.

Specks is down by the field shelter with Whisper and the foals are hanging around by the gate.

"Hey you lot. How are you all today?" I ask as I squeeze myself through the gate.

"Fern and Shadow. Now listen carefully. You need to promise me, to be on your very best behaviour today. Some lovely people are coming to see you and if all goes well, they could well be your own new family as they are willing to give you both your own forever home. According to Aunty, they have a beautiful place which she feels would be perfect for the two of you. How awesome would that be?" I tell them. Both are looking at me as if I have completely lost the plot.

"Morning Specks", I say as she lifts her head up, whilst letting out a little whinny as she makes her way towards me.

"I have a very busy day today my girl. Bella and I are going to a horse show and have entered one of the Show Jumping Classes. I have everything crossed she is going to behave herself", I tell Specks as I gently stroke her beautiful soft neck.

Specks is gently licking my left hand.

"Your tongue is warm and wet. I love the feeling when you lick my hand. It is very therapeutic", I inform her.

"Today we are going to concentrate on grooming you on both sides and see if we can slowly work down your legs. You trust me, don't you girlie?" I ask her.

She is very relaxed as I offer her some nuts. I am sure she is unaware I have already attached the lead rope onto her headcollar.

I place a handful of nuts onto the grass and whilst she is busy eating, I slowly move the body brush over her back and down her hind quarters. Her tail flickers around for a second, so I move the brush back up higher.

"Good girlie", I continue to tell her as I scatter a few more nuts just in front of her.

The body brush glides over her beautiful speckled coat, across her back and down her quarters towards her hock. No reaction. I continue as slowly as I can down her cannon bone towards her fetlock. She shuffles around so I move back up to her neck.

"I know that tickles Specks when I brush your legs, but the more I do it, the quicker you will get used to the feeling", I inform her.

I slowly swap sides and repeat the same with her off-side. She is a little unsure as I touch her hock, so I immediately move back up towards her neck whilst talking to her in a calm and reassuring voice.

"Specks, you are such a brave girl", I tell her as the brush glides down her front leg, down towards her hoof.

Today she doesn't even flinch.

I glance at my watch and cannot believe it is quarter to eight already.

"Come on girlie, let's have a stroll around the field for ten minutes", I tell her as I lightly hold the lead rope.

I start to walk, and I am thrilled to see Specks is right by my side. We head towards the field shelter in unison.

How amazing is this?

Maybe one day it might be possible to lead her over to the sand school?

I am thrilled once again with the progress we have made and offer her a handful of nuts whilst I gently release the lead rope.

"Specks, I have to go now but before I do, I want to tell you how proud I am of you today", I tell her as I wrap my arms around her neck with my cheek against her soft warm neck.

'I just love how she smells, in fact I love everything about her', I think to myself as I gently place a kiss on her velvet like muzzle.

I turn to walk across the field, and I am totally amazed to see Specks is walking closely by my side.

How fabulous is this?

"I really appreciate you kindly escorting me to the gate", I tell her, as I plant one last kiss onto her face.

I have a massive grin on my face as I canter back over to the paddock to get working on making Bella look presentable.

Chapter 37

✳ ✳ ✳

"Morning ems", smiles Freya as she rushes over to give me a hug.

"Are you excited about today? I am. I have butterflies jumping around in my tummy already", she continues.

"To be honest Freya, I haven't had time to give it much thought, but I bet I will start to feel slightly nervous once we get there. Come on let's keep busy, that is the best way of dealing with nerves", I tell her.

"You are right", she replies with a smile.

"I see Bella managed to roll in some poo last night", she laughs.

"I know, I told her she is a little stinker. I am going to ask Aunty if I can put her in one of the spare stables so I can give her a good wash down", I reply.

"Your Aunty is in with Mix and Match. Shall we pop and ask her?" asks Freya.

"Morning Aunty", I say as Freya and I lean over the stable door.

"Hey there my girls. How was your session with Specks?" she enquires.

"Really well thank you. I am not going to tell you too much as I want you to read my notes first", I smile.

"How are Mix and Match today?" asks Freya.

"They both seem very perky today Freya. The pair of them thoroughly enjoyed their breakfast and I am sure the swelling has gone down in little Mix's legs. When you have all left to go off to the show, I will get Jess to help me hose them down. I am not going to turn them out until after Dee has been to see Fern and Shadow as I don't want the two new additions affecting the foal's behaviour", she replies.

"That is a very sensible idea. I did have a word with them earlier and have told them they need to be on their best behaviour", I smile.

"Oh, by the way, Adam messaged me earlier to say a DNA test for two would normally be around one hundred and fifty pounds. He said he is also curious to find out if they are related and therefore has offered a discounted price of seventy-five pounds", she tells us.

"That is really lovely of him. Right Freya, we need to get our thinking caps on. We must somehow raise the money", I smile at her.

"We could have a chat with Jamie later and see if he has any ideas", she beams.

"Great idea", I reply.

"Aunty. Would it be ok to put Bella into one of the spare stables so I can wash her down please?" I ask.

"Of course, Ems, you don't need to ask. It would probably be a lot easier to get them both ready in the stables as you will have a better chance of keeping them clean. I am just going to finish off here and then I will pop to give your Dad a hand getting Crystal ready. I will see you over there", smiles Aunty.

'Eeyore', calls Snowy as we make our way into the paddock.

"Hey little fella. We need to pinch Bella and Hope for a few hours. Is that ok with you?" I ask him as I bend down to give him a kiss.

'Eeyore', he answers back.

Freya and I put Bella and Hope's head collars on and lead them over to the stables where Crystal and Amber are.

We stop to listen as we hear Nicky singing away to Amber in a truly angelic voice.

Freya and I look at each other as she hits the highest note in one of the most beautiful songs, I will always love you, by Whitney Houston.

"Blimey Freya, what a voice she has. I have goose bumps running through my body. Nicky should audition for X-Factor. There aren't many singers around that can carry off a Whitney Houston song so effortlessly', I tell her.

"You are right. She is awesome and should be out there singing to the world", agrees Freya.

Nicky is opening Amber's stable door.

"Morning kiddos. I am so looking forward to today. I just hope I don't make a prat of myself", she laughs.

"Nicky, you have the most amazing singing voice I have ever heard. Freya and I were just saying, you should audition for X-Factor", I reply.

"I am delighted you enjoy my singing but believe it or not I am quite a shy person. I did enter a talent competition a couple of years ago, but I froze and shook like a leaf when I saw the audience and no words would come out", she says in a sad way.

"Oh, I am so sorry to hear that Nicky. It is such a shame for you as your talent seems to be wasted", I tell her.

"I have tried hard to get over my nerves, but to date I haven't found a way. I will keep trying though", she assures us.

"Name a couple of songs and I will sing to you as you get Bella and Hope ready. For some reason, I always feel at ease singing outdoors", she says.

"Maybe you need to enter a talent contest that is held outside? Maybe that could be the answer?" I reply.

"It has to be worth a try", urges Freya.

"Come on, let's get cracking and I promise I will give it some thought.", she smiles.

I start to shampoo the stains from Bella's stunning golden coat. Freya is chatting away to Hope in the next door stable and Nicky is belting out a Shirley Bassey song and wow, I seriously have goose bumps running down my arms once again.

'What a voice, what a talent', I say to myself but once again say it out loud.

"I totally agree, she has the voice of an Angel. I could listen to her singing all day long", smiles Aunty as she pops her head over the stable door.

"Me too", I reply as I start to rinse the shampoo off Bella.

I groom Bella's mane and tail whilst waiting for the wet areas to dry and then get cracking on washing her face, nostrils and under her tail. I work hard as my right hand holds the body brush. It glides over her silky coat as my left hand holds a clean tea towel which I use in between the strokes of my brush. Brush, towel, brush, towel, I continue to repeat this until my arms start to feel like those of an Orangutan. I stand back and look at my beautiful girl with a massive grin on my face. She is shining like a Goddess.

"Oh my, Bella, you do scrub up well", I tell her.

I am sure she's just winked at me again!

"Wow, Bella, don't you look stunning", says Mum as she pops her head over the stable door.

"Bella is shining and glistening like a crystal", she gasps.

"Thanks Mum. What time is it?" I ask.

"Nine-thirty", confirms Mum.

"Really? Where has the time gone? I just need to put some fly spray on Bella, and I will go and fetch Freya and Nicky, so we can nip off to get changed", I reply.

"I have made you all a cup of coffee on the kitchen side and as I knew you probably don't want any breakfast, I have left you all a banana to give you some energy. Make sure you eat it love", says Mum.

"Aw, thanks Mum. You are simply the best. Do you know that?" I grin.

"Right we won't be long Mum, thanks for watching Bella for me", I say as I give her a big hug.

"You are welcome darling. Now off you trot and get changed", she smiles.

Chapter 38

* * *

"I haven't been to a horse show for at least seventeen years. I think the last one I went to was when my beloved Warrior was around sixteen. That was just before he was diagnosed with arthritis at such a young age", says Nicky with a sad tone to her voice.

"It is always good to remember the happy times you spent together. It is only two years since you lost him Nicky and what wonderful memories you have of him", I smile.

"You are right. Come on kiddos, let's get this show on the road", grins Nicky.

Thankfully, the show jacket Freya has lent me, fits like a glove.

Nicky, Freya and I look at each other in utter surprise. It is very unusual for the three of us to look this smart.

"Don't we brush up well, ladies", grins Freya.

We finish the rest of our coffee, trying as hard as we can not to spill any over our clothes and head off quickly to get our tack.

"There you are Ems", says Dad with a smile on his face.

"Now don't you three ladies scrub up well. I almost didn't recognise you", teases Dad.

"Very funny Dad. Are you and Crystal nearly ready?" I ask.

"We are all tacked up and ready to go", he tells us.

'Eeyore, Eeyore', calls Snowy.

"Don't worry about Snowy, he will be fine. I think your Mum is planning to take him into the house again whilst Nicky and your Aunty attend to Mix and Match, however I am not sure your Aunty knows this", he laughs.

"That doesn't surprise me in the least Dad", I grin back.

"I am just popping off to get changed, so I will see you in a jiffy", says Dad.

The three of us carry on our way to get our tack and within ten minutes we are ready to mount our steeds.

"Right you lot, have a great time and I will see you later at the show. I need to go and see what my baby boy is up to", Mum tells us before turning to make her way back to the paddock.

"Wow. Just look at the four of you", beams Jess

"Marks out of ten?" asks Nicky.

"It has to be at least twenty", smiles Jess.

"We are going to have to get cracking", says Freya glancing at her watch.

"Don't forget we are meeting Jamie in ten minutes", she continues.

"I have to say my Pam's Rescue show jumping team are looking very well turned out. In fact, you all look truly awesome. Now make sure you all have fun, ride safely and may the force be with you", Aunty laughs.

"See you later. Good luck with Fern and Shadow", I call as we head off towards the front gates.

To my relief it looks as though it is going to be a cloudy day. It is warm but the forecast is for a maximum temperature of twenty-one degrees which is ideal conditions for our ponies.

Nicky and Dad are riding side by side up front, Freya and I follow closely behind.

"You need to take the next left turn and follow the lane. Jamie lives one hundred yards on the right after the first left hand bend", Freya calls out to Nicky and Dad.

"Got it", Nicky calls back.

What a pretty lane this is. Beech trees stand proudly on either side. I have read these trees are native to southern England and Wales. The thin grey bark is shiny, and the reddish-brown leaves remind me of torpedoes.

I absolutely adore nature. I love the way trees and flowers change through the seasons. I am fascinated by the insects, and small animals that live within the magical woodland alongside so many different species of birds. It is truly amazing how they all live happily within the same vicinity.

"There he is", beams Freya as we see Jamie and Jasmine waiting at the end of a very beautiful and well-maintained driveway.

"Wow, it looks as if we have a fabulous team", grins Jamie.

"Hi Freya, you look very beautiful", he says shyly.

I turn to grin at Freya. She has turned the deepest shade of red in embarrassment but still has a dreamy look in her eyes. I chuckle to myself.

"Hi Jamie, it is a pleasure to meet you. I am Emily's Dad", says Dad as he shakes Jamie's hand.

"I recognise you. Are you Jess or Nicky? I am sure I have seen you once before at Pams", smiles Jamie.

"Once seen, never forgotten eh? I am Nicky and it is great to see you again too", she laughs.

I haven't really had much time to think about the show and now I have, the butterflies are starting to dance.

"Shall Jamie and I lead the way as we don't want to get lost, do we?" suggests Freya.

"Good idea", I reply as Freya rides up to the front as Dad and Nicky drop back.

"I am going to avoid the country route and stick to the roads. That way we can keep our horses reasonably clean for the show. We can come back through the fields on our way back. That way, perhaps we can all have a cheeky canter", grins Jamie.

We all shout "Yes" in unison and laugh with excitement.

Once we have all calmed down, Jamie leads the way and we are last on our way to the show. Freya starts telling Jamie all about Mix and Match and the DNA test.

"Jamie has just come up with a great idea. If any of us are lucky enough to win any prize money today, we think it should go towards Mix and Match's DNA test. Is everyone in?" calls Freya.

"I am not competing, neither is Nicky I don't think, but I am happy to put twenty pounds into the pot", replies Dad.

"I will match that too", grins Nicky.

This is awesome, we already have forty pounds in the pot, which means we only need to raise thirty-five pounds.

Jamie is thrilled to hear Snowy is going home with us and said he has his fingers crossed that all goes well today with Fern and Shadow.

"Only fifteen minutes away", calls Jamie as those naughty butterflies feel like they are now dancing the conga inside my tummy.

Chapter 39

* * *

I GASP AS WE APPROACH the entrance. I have never been to a show this big. There must be hundreds of horses and ponies, some walking, others trotting and lots of whinnying going on.

Bella is busy snorting through her nostrils whilst prancing and dancing around.

"Steady my girl", I tell her as I gently stroke her neck.

"Wow. Look, there are at least six rings", says Freya.

I can see four huge rings roped out, all containing numerous jumps, another ring looks to have gymkhana games laid out ready and the sixth one stands empty at present.

"Who wants to enter the clear round jumping?" asks Jamie looking directly towards us.

"Just Ems and me, and possibly Nicky", replies Freya.

"Me and your Dad are just here to shout you all on Ems. I was going to have a go at doing a clear round, but to be honest I don't feel like I am ready. I hope you don't mind? It is truly awesome just being here. Maybe next time", smiles Nicky.

"We totally understand Nicky. Please don't worry", I reply.

"What about any of the gymkhana classes?" he queries.

"I don't think so Jamie. I will give them a miss this time", I reply.

"No way Ems. Don't be a spoilsport. Come on please. I dare you", she grins.

"Go on Ems, it will be fun", urges Dad.

"I am not sure, especially after what happened in practice yesterday", I say reluctantly.

"Don't be a wuss Ems. How about walk, trot, canter, lead? Go on pretty please", she begs with a big grin on her face.

"Ok, you win. I just hope we are not in the same heat as I don't trust you", I smile back.

"Coolio", laughs Freya.

"Let me get this right. Freya, you are going to enter the fourteen two and under class, the clear round jumping and walk, trot, canter, lead? Ems you are doing the same?" he asks.

"Correct", we blurt out at precisely the same time.

"Why don't I go and register as there is bound to be a queue, I can pick up your numbers and meet you over by the warm up ring", he tells us.

"That would be great Jamie, as long as you don't mind", Freya replies warmly.

"Here is my entry money", I say as I hand him a twenty-pound note.

"Here's mine too", replies Freya as she hands him her note.

They touch hands and for a slight moment, the two of them seem to be in a world of their own as they look dreamingly into each-other's eyes.

"See you all shortly", smiles Jamie as he and Jasmine make their way to the registration tent.

Freya is glowing the brightest shade of red again.

I smile to myself, it is wonderful to see her so happy.

"Come on then, let's go and find the warm up area", says Freya.

Everyone seems to be so friendly. Whenever we ride past anyone, they immediately smile and say hello. I must say, I am thrilled to see so many male riders today and I notice there are a lot of barefoot ponies too.

I start to relax a little. I know I need to concentrate on staying as calm as possible for Bella's sake.

The three of us follow Freya through the crowds until we arrive at the ringside.

I glance at my watch to see it is only ten forty-five.

I wonder what time our classes will start?

"Loose pony", calls out the commentator.

I look all around but cannot see one. My eyes are drawn to the most beautiful Andalusian horse I have ever seen. He is pure white with a hint of grey dappling. The flawless white mane flows all the way down to his shoulder. He walks in a very majestic manner, and every single stride he takes looks completely effortless. He truly is a most outstanding specimen and a true credit to his breed.

A stunning chestnut Arab, with four white socks, and a very unusual head is walking towards me. I have never seen a marking this unusual. One side of his face is chestnut and the other side white. He has certainly attracted my attention as I smile and say good morning to his rider.

"Here we are. All done", says Jamie's voice bringing my attention back to the job in hand.

"Ems, your number is one hundred and eighty-eight. Freya you are one hundred and eighty-nine and I am one hundred and ninety", smiles Jamie as he hands them over to us.

"The gymkhana classes start at eleven am, so any minute now. The egg and spoon will be first, followed by the sack race and the walk, trot, canter, lead is next. We need to keep an ear out for the commentator's announcements. Your jumping class starts at one o'clock in ring two. My class starts at one-fifteen in ring three. I hope somehow we are going to be able to watch each other jump", he continues.

"Hopefully Mum and Jess will be here before our classes", I reply.

"I will message Jess now to tell her what time you are jumping along with the ring number", says Nicky.

"Guess what?" beams Freya.

"Mum and my brother are coming over to cheer us on", she continues before any of us have any chance to answer.

"That is truly fabulous Freya. It will be lovely to see your Mum again and to finally meet your little brother at last", I grin back.

"Who would like a drink?" asks Dad.

"Now that sounds like a great idea", Nicky says.

"Would one of you hold Crystal whilst I pop and get us some drinks please?" asks Dad.

"I will come and give you a hand, that is if you wouldn't mind holding Jasmine for me Freya", smiles Jamie.

"It will be my pleasure", replies Freya as she effortlessly slides off Hope to take a hold of Jasmines reins.

I jump off Bella and take Crystal's reins as Dad makes a note of our drink orders on his iPhone.

"Jamie really is a gentleman", I say to Freya.

"I know he is. Aren't I lucky?" she grins back.

"By the way, I keep meaning to ask you. I hope you behaved yourself last night when Joseph gave you a lift home?" I ask her.

"Of course, I did. I decided ages ago, he is way too old for me and then I met Jamie", she smiles.

"Look at that stunner", pipes out Nicky.

We turn to where she is pointing.

A vision of beauty lies ahead. I watch as a striking black and white Gypsy Vanner strolls by. His mane is half black from the top of his ears, then halfway down it turns pure white. His forelock reaches all the way down to his muzzle as it bounces up and down with every stride he takes.

"Wow. Now if I were to ever own another horse, that one would most definitely be the one for me. Did you know the Gypsy Vanner horse's genes were created with the help of the Shire horse, Clydesdale and the Dales pony?" asks Nicky.

"No. I didn't know that. How very interesting. I must say they do look a tough and hardy type of horse too", I reply.

"There we go, love", says Dad as he hands me a cup of coffee.

"Thanks Dad", I reply.

"All entrants for the sack race. Please make your way to ring one in ten minutes", calls the commentator.

"It will be me and you in the next race Ems", grins Freya.

"Come on then, we had better head over there and do some warming up", I reply.

Chapter 40

* * *

BELLA WARMS UP BEAUTIFULLY AND is responding to everything I ask of her. I ride over to ring one and tell the lady my number. There looks to be quite a lot of entries and a few smaller ponies taking part too.

I am called over to stand in line with the other five entrants. I glance around to look for Freya to see she has been allocated to the third group.

"Now don't forget, you must wait until I shout the word go. If you trot when you should be walking, you must turn a circle. The same goes if you canter when you are trotting. If you don't follow the rules, I am afraid, you will be disqualified. The first two to finish will go into the final round. Right is everyone ready? On your marks, get set, go", says the starter.

I am in lane one and Bella is walking beautifully.

"Good girlie, just keep walking like you are Bella", I say to her.

I am sure out of the corner of my eye I notice the pony in the next lane turning in a circle. I need to focus. It is time for us to trot and I urge Bella forward. She takes one stride into a canter so we need to do a circle which we do as fast as we can.

"Steady girlie", I say to her.

It is time to turn and get ready to canter back and we are off. Bella is covering the ground beautifully. I jump off, pull the reins over her head and run as fast as I can to the finish. I stop and bend over clutching my sides as I try to get my breath back.

Number two hundred and forty-six and number one hundred and eighty-eight, congratulations you are through to the final.

That is my number I realise as I proceed to give Bella a huge well-done hug.

"Wow Ems. Well done you and Bella. You were only an inch away from beating the winner", grins Dad.

We watch heat two, which appears to be a complete disaster. Nearly every pony at some point is compelled to turn in a circle. In fact, it looks as though they are waltzing!

Heat three is about to start and Freya is in lane two.

They are off.

Hope is walking forward beautifully, she looks to be in third place as Freya turns and asks Hope to trot. She is still in third place as she turns, and urges Hope into a canter.

"Come on Freya", Jamie and I shout out loudly.

Hope must be responding to our voices. They make the final turn, Freya is now in second place as she runs for all she is worth towards the finishing line.

I know I shouldn't laugh but what happens next looked very funny, just like something you would see a clown do in an acrobatic show.

It looked as though Freya has tripped on something as she lands on her knees whilst trying to keep hold of Hope who was prancing around showing off. I watch aghast as one of her jodhpur boots flies across the grass behind her.

Poor Freya.

"Are you ok?" asks Jamie in a concerned voice.

"I am, thank you. My right boot caught the heel on my left one and that was it, game over", she replies.

"Bad luck Freya", I say. "Sorry for laughing but you looked like an acrobat, I didn't know you had a hidden talent" I chuckle.

"Here's a little joke to cheer you up, Freya, "says Dad. "A little boy was standing in the classroom crying. The teacher asked him what was wrong. "I can't find my boots," the little boy sobbed. The teacher looked around the room and saw a pair of boots. "Are these yours?" she asked. "No, those aren't mine," he cried. The teacher and the little boy searched all over the classroom for his boots. Finally, the teacher gave up and said, "Are you SURE those aren't your boots?" "Yes, I'm sure," sobbed the boy. "Mine had snow on them!"

The laughter starts and it is great to see Freya looking back to her normal cheerful self.

Well done Dad.

"Off you go and all the best of British", grins Dad as I am called along with the other seven to take my place in the final.

I have been allocated lane seven. The rider to my right is on a beautiful grey Arab.

"On your marks, get set, get ready, go", says the starter.

We are off.

"That's right Bella. Walking, walking, good girl", I tell her as I concentrate on looking ahead. We turn. "Trotting, trotting, trotting", good girlie. We turn. "Go Bella", I say as we fly to the other end like a flash of lightning. I leap out of the saddle, throw the reins off her head and run as fast as I can to the finish. We made it. Bella and I come to a standstill and I lean forwards as I try to get my breath back again.

"And the winner is number seventy-two. In second place number one hundred and eighty-eight", she calls.

I don't hear the rest of what the caller says as I cannot believe we have come second.

"Bella, Bella, Bella, you did it, my baby. We came second. I am so proud of you", I tell her as I wrap my arms tightly around her.

"Could the first four come forward to get your rosettes please?" asks the caller.

I mount Bella in a flash and stand proudly as we receive our beautiful three tier, silky blue rosette. I can vaguely hear Dad, Nicky, Freya and Jamie cheering close by. I am also handed a little white envelope. I open it up and I am totally surprised to see a ten-pound note. I didn't have a clue there were cash prizes for the gymkhana. Ten pounds towards Mix and Match's DNA. What a fabulous bonus.

My cheeks literally ache from grinning as Bella and I make our way out of the ring.

"I bet you are glad I dared you to enter the class now Ems, aren't you? Well done to you both", beams Freya as the others proceed to congratulate us.

Chapter 41

✳ ✳ ✳

"SHALL WE POP OVER AND have a go at the clear round jumping before our classes start?" asks Jamie.

"Great idea", I reply.

I am really looking forward to this now. I feel as though I am on cloud nine.

Jamie offers to go first.

The four of us watch in awe as he and Jasmine clear jump after jump after jump. It is so effortless, what a true bond the pair of them have.

"Wow. That was awesome", I call as we all start clapping as he picks up his rosette.

"I am so proud of you and Jasmine", beams Freya. "I am also relieved you are not in our class", she continues.

"There you are", we hear the familiar voices of Mum and Jess.

"I hope we are not too late love?" asks Mum as she gives me a kiss and then one for Dad.

"Perfect timing Mum", I say as I proceed to push my rosette in front of her face.

They both seemed thrilled for me and Bella and are sorry they missed my race.

"Wish me luck", smiles Freya as she and Hope set off into the ring.

What a truly fabulous display, totally magical to watch as they clear each jump in a very controlled manner.

We clap as hard as we can as she returns proudly with her clear round rosette.

"What a fabulous round Freya", I say as she holds out her hand for a high five.

"Aunty would have been so proud if she had seen the two of you jump like that", I continue.

"Don't worry. Pam will be able to see it as I have recorded every moment on my phone. Well done Freya, you were amazing", grins Jamie.

What a good idea of Jamie's. I wouldn't have thought of that.

"By the way, I recorded you and Bella in the gymkhana class too Ems. I will send it across to you later when I have wi-fi so you can show your Mum", he smiles.

"Fabulous, so I will be able to watch it after all. What a good lad you are Jamie", smiles Mum.

"Your turn Ems. Bella has had plenty of warm up, so just remember to concentrate and breathe", informs Freya.

I salute her as we make our way into the ring.

The jumps are set at a maximum of two foot six and there are ten in total.

Bella and I canter around the outside towards the start.

"Slowly girlie", I say in a soft voice as we head to the first jump.

Bella clears it by at least a foot, and we continue straight onto the next one. We are safely over. I ask Bella to go slowly around the bend as we approach the double, she is feeling relaxed and collected. Over we go, one stride two strides, clear. Over the next we fly like a bird. I collect her up and ease her back, and I am in total control as we head towards the treble.

"Slowly Bella", I ask her as she takes a strong hold.

Here we go. Bella has hold of the bit and has taken matters into her own hands. All I can do is sit tight and trust her. One, two, three, clear. I let out a sigh of relief as I ease her back. I regain some control as we clear jump eight. We are now on the homeward stretch, just two more left.

Bella is fighting for her head once again.

"Bella slowly", I tell her, but once again she isn't listening.

Bella has her head in the air and is literally flying towards the last two jumps.

"Off you go", I say to her, as to be honest, I don't have a lot of choice.

Jump nine, jump ten, I cannot believe we have a clear round.

I canter her on a circle and bring her down to trot, then eventually to walk. Bella is huffing and puffing out of sheer excitement, and so am I.

"Thank you", I say slightly out of breath as I take my rosette from the lovely lady.

"Blimey Ems. You made my blood pressure rise watching that", says Freya.

"I think mine is high too", I manage to reply.

"Before the main class, I think you need to get a bit more of that energy out of Bella. Once you have got your breath back and we have all had a drink, maybe we should head over to the warm up ring and do some groundwork?" asks Freya.

"Let's go over there now. We can do some transitional work, I can cool her down a bit, then we can have something to eat?" I suggest.

"Great idea" Freya says.

After a while, we leave the warm up ring to go and find the others.

"There you are, you two. I have bought a flask of coffee, tea and some sandwiches", announces Mum.

"Oh, how wonderful", I reply as I slide out of my saddle onto slightly wobbly legs.

"Come on, tuck in", she says, as she carefully lays it all out onto a blanket.

We loosen our ponies' girths and let them graze.

After we have filled our tummies with our favourite sandwiches and drinks, Freya suddenly jumps up.

"I can't believe it is only fifteen minutes until our class", exclaims Freya.

"Come on Ems. We need to go and warm up again", she continues.

"I will catch you up", smiles Jamie who is finishing off his cheese and salad sandwiches which Mum has made for him.

Chapter 42

* * *

"Hurry up ems. They are calling our numbers out", says Freya excitedly.

We bump into Jamie as we leave the warm up ring and he wishes us both luck and we say the same back.

I am delighted to hear me and Bella, are third on the list but unfortunately for Freya, she is number twenty. Thirty-seven are taking part so this could take a while.

The first rider receives four faults and the next one three faults.

"May the force be with you", says Freya, as Bella and I enter the ring.

The bells rings and we are ready to go.

Bella and I are in complete harmony as we clear all ten jumps with me fully in control. I am absolutely delighted and so is everyone else. We leave the ring and I have a massive cheesy grin across my face.

Thirty minutes later and it is Freya and Hope's turn.

What a truly fabulous performance as they also complete a clear round.

We are both going to be in the jump offs!

Jamie has been drawn twenty-two of thirty-nine entries and he is the next one in.

The jumps are a lot higher than ours and he makes it look so easy and Jamie manages to get a well-deserved clear round too.

Now we need to wait patiently to see how many make it through to compete again.

It is two-thirty by the time commentator calls seven of us back into the ring for our jump off.

There are still five more to jump in Jamie's class.

They decide to send us in, in the order of who jumped clear.

Yikes, me and Bella are first.

"Bella, I love you with every ounce of my heart. Come on we can do this. Let's just enjoy ourselves", I tell her with a pat down her neck.

The bell rings and the clock start's ticking.

Off we go.

Bella glides over the three-foot parallel, and we head towards the false wall. She clips the top with her hind leg, I immediately look back and I am relieved to see it hasn't fallen off. I take a gentle tug as we go towards the double. This feels truly magical and I am in full control as we fly over with ease. Now for the next, another parallel. We sail over effortlessly. I know the treble is next, but I also know we are riding against the clock.

What would you do?

"Come on baby let's go for it", I tell her as I soften my hands a little and push Bella further forward. We are over the treble in a jiffy. I gather her back into me and she responds as we turn towards the last two jumps.

"Go on baby. It is all yours", I tell her once again. She immediately responds and we jump them both with ease.

We are clear.

I cannot believe it as I gently pull Bella up and look towards Freya, grinning like the Cheshire cat from Alice in wonderland.

"A very well done to Bella and Emily. You have a clear round and have recorded a fabulous time of fifty-two point four seconds. Could we have Freya and Hope next into the ring please", says the commentator.

The adrenalin is pumping through my body and I feel a little bit shaky. I am so proud of Bella's performance. Now we need to sit tight and see what happens.

"Ems, that was literally awesome to watch. Bella is an absolute star against the clock. She has a terrific turn of foot", Freya congratulates us as she rides Hope into the ring.

"Good luck", I call.

"Amazing", says Mum with a big grin across her face.

"By the way, there are nine to jump in total in Jamie's jump offs", she continues.

We watch in delight as Freya and Hope complete a steady clear round with a time of fifty-nine point three seconds.

Freya has an enormous grin across her face and pats Hope's neck proudly as they leave the ring.

Only five more to go. Fingers crossed.

I have to say I am still feeling slightly shaky as I jump off Bella whilst trying to keep my legs from trembling.

The next rider unfortunately knocks off the top pole on the first parallel.

Rider four completes a clear round in fifty-seven point two seconds.

I am slightly worried when I see rider five is on board the beautiful chestnut Arab we saw earlier, the one with the two-toned face.

I hold my breath as the two of them skip over the jumps with ease. What a fabulous performance and they truly deserve to have taken the lead in fifty seconds dead.

Rider six unfortunately gets a refusal.

Freya and I grip hands as we watch the last finalist.

The stunning black pony is really on his toes. His rider is struggling to hold him as they jump the first five clear at a very fast pace. I can see they are going too fast towards the treble and the pony literally barges through them as if they aren't there. They pull up and retire from the ring.

"And in first place we have Chloe and Benjy. In second place Emily and Bella. In third place Blake and Wendy and in fourth place Freya and Hope", we hear the commentator announce.

"OMG, OMG", we both say jumping up and down on the spot like a pair of crazy people.

"We are so proud of you", beams Mum. "Come on quickly, get back in the ring", she cries.

My hands are literally shaking as I grin across at Dad, Nicky and Jess.

Freya is just about to remount when her Mum and brother appear.

"I didn't think you were coming", cries Freya as she wraps her arms tightly around her Mum.

"Well done Sis", says the boy who I am assuming is her brother Lewis, as he joins in the group hug too.

"We have been watching you all day darling. I thought it was better for us to keep our distance as we didn't want to put you under any extra pressure. You will not believe how proud I am of you", she continues as tears of happiness roll down her face.

I cannot help it and feel choked up too. This is going to mean so much to Freya.

"Come on Freya", I urge.

"We need to go and collect our rosettes", I tell her.

"I am coming", beams Freya as she literally catapults herself onto Hope and we make our way back into the ring.

Bella and I stand proudly as we are congratulated and handed our second blue rosette of the day along with another small envelope. I watch closely as Freya receives a beautiful green rosette and tenderly pats Hope. She has a massive grin on her face.

Now for our lap of honour. The crowd clap and cheer as the four of us and our ponies canter proudly around the entire ring. This is another moment I want to last forever.

Eventually, we pull up to a walk and Freya immediately rides across to me to give me a massive high five.

"Quickly", calls Mum.

"Jamie's just about to go in for the jump off", she continues.

We ride across as quickly as we can.

Jamie looks over his shoulder, sees Freya watching him and grins.

He and Jasmine are off.

The pair of them look to be on a mission as he urges Jasmine forward, they clear the first jump with ease, he collects her up before he urges her forward and they complete the whole course with a clear round in forty-nine seconds flat.

"And the winner is Jamie riding Jasmine who have achieved the fastest time of the day", says the commentator.

The rest of what she says is a complete blur as Freya and I jump off our ponies and dance around crazily once again.

"OMG, OMG", repeats Freya.

Mum, Dad, Nicky, Jess Freya's Mum and brother are clapping and cheering as loud as they can.

We all watch with sheer delight as Jamie and Jasmine lead the other three for their lap of honour. He is wearing his beautiful red sash, and Jasmine is wearing her stunning four tier red rosette. They canter around the ring with Jamie holding out his fabulous silver cup for all the spectators to see.

Honestly, when I woke up this morning, I didn't have a clue this was going to happen.

Chapter 43

* * *

JAMIE PROUDLY RIDES OUT OF the ring and has a very well-deserved grin across his face. He is smiling directly at Freya.

"Jamie, you were truly amazing. What a display you put up", Freya gushes as he slides off Jasmine to give her a massive hug and a kiss on her cheek.

Freya is glowing with pure happiness.

"Your Aunty is going to be over the moon when she hears all about your fabulous achievements today", grins Nicky.

"Oh yes, I nearly forgot", I say as I open the white envelope.

I am delighted to see thirty pounds looking back at me.

"Don't forget I have an envelope too", smiles Jamie.

"Freya would you open it for me?" he asks.

"I would be delighted to", she smiles back as she takes the envelope from him.

"Wow, fifty smackaroonies", announces Freya.

"Smackaroonies?" enquires Jamie laughing.

"Pounds, smackaroonies is my other word for pounds", Freya giggles in response.

"Are you sure you still want to donate the fifty pounds Jamie? We've already raised enough money to pay for Mix and Match's DNA?" I ask him.

"Don't be silly Ems. We made a pact and I am delighted my winnings will go towards Pam's pony rescue", he smiles back.

"Let's have a count up", grins Freya.

"Jess can you give Freya twenty pounds please", says Nicky.

"Love, can you do the same", Dad says to Mum.

Nicky and Mum hand the money to Freya and I give her what I have from my two envelopes.

"Fifty, eighty, ninety, one hundred and ten, one hundred and thirty pounds", she announces in glee.

"That gives Aunty an extra fifty-five pounds profit after paying for the DNA test", I say in delight.

"Well done team Pam's pony rescues", grins Mum.

"I am so proud of all of you and I am so pleased I rode over with you today. It really has been great being back in the saddle", grins Dad.

"Right. I need to make tracks now as I need to get cracking on the Sunday roast. Nicky, Jess, Sharon, Jamie and Lewis, would you like to join us? I have prepared plenty and it would be lovely to have you all join us, as we go home tomorrow", smiles Mum.

"I would have loved to, but I have my Nan and Grandad coming over. I truly appreciate the invite though", says Jamie.

"Oh Mum, please say yes", smiles Freya.

"We would love to, wouldn't we Lewis?" smiles Sharon as Jake nods in agreement.

"It would be rude not to, wouldn't it Jess?" smiles Nicky.

"Most definitely. I can give you a hand too, as I absolutely love to cook", smiles Jess.

"That would be a great help love", Mum replies to Jess.

"Come on then, let's get cracking. Dinner will be ready on the table for six-thirty prompt. Sharon and Lewis, we will see you back at Pam's", she continues.

"Ride safely and we will see you later", calls Jess, as she and Mum, say their goodbyes.

I cannot believe it is four-fifteen already.

"Bella, I am so proud of you baby and so glad we came. What fabulous fun we have had today", I tell her as I hold her tight as she leans her head into my back.

"Right. Shall we see if our ponies need a drink and then set off home?" asks Freya.

"Good idea", I reply as we lead our mounts over to the large black bins.

Bella looks to be blowing bubbles. She snorts as the water splashes on her face and she curls up her top lip in the air as if she is laughing again.

The ride home goes quickly as we chat about the wonderful time we have had at the show. We of course cannot resist giving Freya a little bit of stick about her jodhpur boot flying off.

We all decided not to canter on the way home. The ponies have worked hard enough so we just all enjoy a nice and relaxed walk home.

"Thank you for a fabulous day. Freya I will text you later", smiles Jamie as he heads off up his driveway.

We all say our goodbyes before heading off back to Auntys.

Chapter 44

AUNTY IS WAITING PATIENTLY AT the gates with a very large grin across her face.

"My word, Freya and you have made me so very proud, today Ems. So has Jamie and I will tell him so when I see him next. Your Mum has given me the money you have collected. I love the lot of you", says Aunty with tears of pride streaming down her face.

"We will tell you all about our day later Aunty. How did it go with Fern and Shadow?" I ask, quickly changing the subject.

Aunty immediately composes herself.

"Well, the family were absolutely lovely just like Bev had told me. Fern and Shadow were so gentle with their children. It was love at first sight for everyone. Dee even brought her thoroughbred in their horsebox. Whilst Snowy was once again in the kitchen with your Mum, we introduced the three of them in the paddock and after cantering around for a while, they all settled down to graze as if they had been together forever. After a long chat, we all decided it would be better for Dee and her family to take Fern and Shadow home with them today on a two-week trial. They are totally committed, and I must say, scored brownie points by bringing their horse here with them. As we have our two new arrivals, it made sense", smiles Aunty.

"That is fabulous news Aunty. I am so happy for them", I grin.

"I didn't get to say goodbye", says Freya in a sad voice.

"Don't worry Freya. I had already thought about that. I have asked Bev if you can go with her to see them in two weeks-time to complete the paperwork, and she has agreed", replies Aunty.

Freya now has a very big grin across her face.

"What about Mix and Match? How are they doing?" I ask.

"They are doing great. Mix was as good as gold when we hosed her legs down. Jess and I led them slowly over to the field and they immediately settled down to graze alongside Juno, Trixy and Misty", she replies.

'Eeyore', Snowy calls in the distance.

Bella whinnies back to her brother whilst pawing her front near hoof along the floor.

"Don't be so impatient", I tell her.

"She is right, we have been standing here chatting too long. Come on, I will give Nicky and bro a hand to get my girls untacked", says Aunty.

"See you two girls back at the house", she calls as she trots off ahead.

Snowy is waiting for us as we walk towards the paddock.

'Eeyore, Eeyore', he calls loudly.

Bella whinnies back and so does Hope. As soon as we get into the paddock, Bella and Snowy nuzzle each other in greeting. We untack and give Hope and Bella a groom, they each have a carrot and the three of them settle happily down to graze.

They must be very tired from all the hard work they have done today. I cannot tell you how proud I am feeling.

Six thirty on the dot and I count nine of us sitting around Aunty's kitchen table. Mum and Jess have excelled as they serve up one of the best Sunday dinners I have ever tasted.

Suki, Moss, Molly, Lexy and Sugar have a mini roast dinner too in their food bowls and Tinker has one tailored just for him.

I look around and smile to myself. I can see eight very happy faces.

I am going to miss Mum, Dad and Suki when they go home tomorrow. I bet Dad would much rather stay here than having to go back to work.

"I would like to make a toast to go with the roast", announces Dad as he stands up holding his glass of wine.

"This toast is for my wonderful sister Pam. Sis, I want you to know how proud I am of all the fantastic rescue work you do. Seeing it with my own eyes and being involved over this weekend has been a real eye-opener for me. You have a very special place here with such wonderful people surrounding you. You are passionate and full of drive and aspire to help any animal in need. I will promise you now, I am going to be more supportive with your work in the future and I feel honoured to have you as my sister", announces Dad with a slight croak to his voice.

Everyone raises their glass high into the air.

"Cheers Sis", says Dad as he clinks everyone's glass one by one as he makes his way around the table.

You have guessed it, Aunty has tears of happiness streaming down her face.

'I really am going to have to buy Aunty some more hankies' I think to myself.

As Dad goes to toast her glass, Aunty gets up from her chair. I watch feeling slightly emotional as they hug each other tight.

Aunty remains standing up as Dad releases her gently from his great big bear hug.

"For once, I am totally lost for words. Thank you", says Aunty as the tears continue to roll down her cheeks.

"Why don't you and Freya show Lewis around whilst we clear up the dishes" says Mum.

"We don't mind helping", I reply.

"No, go on, off you trot. We can manage", smiles Mum.

We didn't need telling twice and make our way out of the kitchen as quickly as we can.

Lewis is in awe of Snowy. I have to say what a lovely boy he is, for a ten-year old. He is very well behaved and has perfect manners. Freya is so good with him and has the patience of a saint as he fires question after question at her.

It is eight-thirty by the time Sharon, Freya, Lewis, Jess and Nicky leave to go home.

Everyone has had a truly awesome time and I must say I am starting to feel totally exhausted. It has been such a long day.

I excuse myself whilst Mum, Dad and Aunty open another bottle of wine and get to work typing up today's notes.

It is ten-thirty before my head hits my comfy and much needed pillow. I cannot believe I have already been here for one full week and a day. I only have thirteen days left now at Auntys.

'I wonder what next week will bring?' I think, as I try hard to stop my eyes from closing.

TO BE CONTINUED

40838890R00123

Made in the USA
Middletown, DE
01 April 2019